THE

kekla magoon

NEW YORK
LONDON
TORONTO
SYDNEY

ALADDIN

ALADDIN PAPERBACKS

An imprint of Simon & Schuster Children's Publishing Division

1230 Avenue of the Americas, New York, NY 10020

Copyright © 2009 by Kekla Magoon

All rights reserved, including the right of reproduction
in whole or in part in any form.

ALADDIN and related logo are registered trademarks of
Simon & Schuster, Inc.

Designed by Karin Paprocki

The text of this book was set in Cochin.

Manufactured in the United States of America

First Aladdin edition January 2009

2 4 6 8 10 9 7 5 3

Library of Congress Cataloging-in-Publication Data

Magoon, Kekla.

The rock and the river / by Kekla Magoon. — 1st Aladdin ed.

p.   cm.

Summary: In 1968 Chicago, fourteen-year-old Sam Childs
is caught in a conflict between his father's nonviolent approach
to seeking civil rights for African Americans and his older brother,
who has joined the Black Panther Party.

[1. Civil rights movements—Fiction. 2. Black Panther Party—Fiction.
3. Racism—Fiction. 4. Brothers—Fiction. 5. African Americans—Fiction.
6. United States—History—20th century—Fiction.] I. Title.

PZ7.M2739Ro 2009 / 2008029170 / [Fic]—dc22

ISBN-13: 978-1-4169-7582-3 / ISBN-10: 1-4169-7582-9

for
KOBI

CHAPTER 1

I TRIED TO PRETEND I WAS SOMEWHERE ELSE. The long morning of marching was stretching into an even longer afternoon of standing still. It was a peaceful protest; orderly and insistent, like the ticking of a clock. Just the way Father always wanted. He stood up at the front of the throng, feeding the crowd with his words. The podium shook under the pounding of his fist. Mama stood behind him, where she always stood, hands folded, lashes low, her stillness a mirror for his fervor. On either side of them, Ty and Jerry, Father's security team, looked like twin linebacker mountains.

The crowd spread away from the courthouse steps and filled two city blocks—but that was nothing. I'd been to marches that filled ten. The crowd was heated as always, but the warmth didn't reach inside me. The February air had me shivering. I pulled my coat tighter and leaned into my brother.

Above us, the Chicago skyline loomed against gray clouds. Rough concrete pillars stood proud above the courthouse steps, looking weathered and bored, like they were tired of carrying the weight of the law on their shoulders. Just staring at the pillars made me want to rest. With my fingertip in the air and one eye closed, I traced the line of the rooftops. I closed my ears to whatever Father was saying. Chances were, I'd heard it before.

News cameramen pushed past us to the front of the barricades, shouting, "Coming through," as they tromped on toes and threw elbows. All their cameras pointed at Father. I was glad to be away from the glaring lenses.

People shifted around me. Everyone's space invaded everyone else's, and the ripple effect separated me from my brother.

"Stick," I called, grabbing for his arm. My fingers brushed his sleeve.

Stick turned. "What?"

A couple of people pushed between us. Suddenly I hated the crowds, hated the way everyone pressed up against one another. My heart beat in rhythm with the swaying of shoulders in front of me; out of control.

Stick pushed through to stand beside me. "What is it, Sam?" he asked.

"Nothing, never mind." I couldn't explain it. And I

couldn't say I'd gotten scared for no reason. That might have been okay when I was little, but not at thirteen. I'd just rather have been anywhere else than the middle of this street on a cold, wet Saturday afternoon.

Stick stared at me. After a moment, he grinned. "What, you wanna bail?"

"Yeah," I said, rolling my eyes. "Right." Not even Stick had ever dared leave in the middle of one of Father's demonstrations.

The crowd pressed in, driving us even farther from the podium.

"Just say the word, my man. They'll never miss us."

I shook my head. Tempting, but impossible.

The crowd lurched forward. "That's right!" they yelled, in answer to something Father said. I tuned in for a second. He was up to the part about how it was 1968, we'd come so far but had so much further to go . . . and on and on.

So here we all were.

Here we'd all been for as long as I could remember.

I was tired of marching, of protesting. Of leaning my back against a wall and expecting the wall to move. I wanted to rest.

"Stick," I said. "I want to go home."

"I know," he said. "I know." I shivered and glanced around. Stick smiled and slung his arm across my shoulders.

The thick wall of his coat sleeve warmed my ears. "I can take the heat if you can," he said.

Father would see us leave. He had this uncanny sixth sense—he always knew when we disobeyed him. There'd be hell to pay. But, right then, I didn't care. Just once, I wanted to do something unexpected.

"Let's get out of here," I said.

Stick grinned. "That's my boy," he said, thumping my shoulder. Stick liked to shake things up. I always followed the rules and did what I was supposed to. Still, I was so cold, and tired of leaning against this wall. Father would say, you get enough people to lean, and the wall will move. I used to believe it, but I just wasn't sure anymore.

"C'mon," Stick said. He plowed through the crowd. I followed, grabbing the back of his coat and stumbling in his wake. The cheers rose above us as we moved farther and farther from Father's stage.

Then, different sounds surfaced amid the crowd's claps and cheering. Grunting. The thumping of fist to flesh. Fight sounds. Stick slowed.

"What the hell?" he shouted. He tore out of my grip and rushed forward. A group of white men armed with bats, bottles, and sticks were beating on people at the edge of the crowd. The protesters cried out and shielded themselves with their arms.

Stick burst forward and grabbed one of the white men, pulling him off a gray-haired woman who dropped, crying, to the ground. The man slammed an elbow into Stick's bony chest. Stick groaned, then grabbed the man by the hair and punched him in the face.

People bumped me from all sides, but I couldn't move. Several protesters had fallen to the ground, and two came crawling toward me, scrambling to get out of the way.

"We will walk hand in hand," Father's voice intoned above the fray. "We will push forward step by step until they see the truth: that all men are created equal, and should be equal under the law." I turned to look toward Father, but three helmeted cops were pushing their way through the crowd to get to the fight.

"Stick! The cops!" I shouted. His head snapped up. In that split second, the man fighting with him bent down and seized the neck of a broken bottle from the ground. "No!" I cried. The man swung and the bottle connected with Stick's temple. Stick fell to the ground, and the man stumbled away.

I grabbed Stick's shoulders. His forehead was bleeding, but he sat up and took my hand.

"We've got to get out of here," I said as the cops drew closer. The mass of people parted to let them through.

Stick and I glanced at each other, then I pulled him up and we bolted the other way. When the cops came, it wouldn't matter who had started it. It would always be us up against the bricks.

We ran several blocks, ducking around corners until the sounds of the crowd faded behind us. I was ready to run all the way home, if I had to.

"Wait." Stick stopped and leaned his arm against the side of a building. He bent over, breathing hard. I circled around. "Far enough," he huffed. But Stick could run farther and faster than anyone I knew, certainly than me.

The gash on Stick's forehead dripped blood over his brow and along his cheek. He swiped the thick red stream away from his eye with the back of his wrist.

"I think we have to go to the hospital," I said, looking closer at his head. "There might be glass in there, or gravel." One of Chicago's main hospitals was four or five blocks away, down toward the lakefront.

"It's fine," he said, but he swayed and leaned back against the building.

"It's not fine." I took his arm and put it over my shoulders. "Come on."

I walked Stick in through the emergency entrance. The doors slid open for us, and the steady bustle of the city streets gave way to the squeak of gurney wheels and the impatient chattering of waiting people.

People stared as we passed. There was a lot of blood now. On Stick, and on me, where he had leaned his head against me while we walked. Our shirts were stained red at the shoulders.

We approached the main desk. Two blond nurses stood behind the long, curved counter, talking. They looked up at us.

"What happened?" the younger nurse asked.

"He—had an accident," I said. "A few blocks from here."

The older nurse studied Stick's forehead, then looked back at me. Her eyes seemed to hover over the rim of her glasses.

"A few blocks from here?" she asked, her tone skeptical. "You protesting?"

"Yes, ma'am. He fell and hit his head. In the crowd."

She pressed her lips together and the bun of hair atop her head appeared to tighten. "Well, you'll just have to wait," she said, crossing thin arms over her chest. "We're full right now." She bent forward and neatened a stack of papers on the desk.

The young nurse fiddled with the edge of her uniform pocket. Then she smoothed her hands over her full hips and spoke timidly. "I could take him to—"

"Have a seat in the chairs. Someone will be with you shortly."

I started to move back toward the waiting area, but Stick shifted his weight and locked his arm tighter around me, keeping us in place. "Ask how long," he murmured against my ear.

"How long will it take?" I asked.

She didn't look up from her charts. "We'll call you."

"Is there a waiting list?" I said, addressing the young nurse this time. Her clear blue gaze reassured me somehow. "How many people are ahead of us?" I added. Stick grunted approval.

The young nurse came around the desk and laid her hand against Stick's cheek. She tilted his head gently to get a better look. "Well," she said. "We need to get you washed up and stop this bleeding.

"I'll find a place for you, honey," she added softly, avoiding the other nurse's eye. She rolled a wheelchair out from behind the desk and motioned Stick to sit in it. Then she pushed him away down a long hall and into a room. I started to follow.

"You wait right here," the other nurse said. I turned back. She peered at me over her glasses; her eyes sharpened on me like a bird of prey spying a mouse.

"Where are your parents? You should call them." She frowned.

"They're still at the demonstration."

"Why weren't you with them?" she asked, eyebrows folding low. I shrugged. No point in trying to explain.

"Come with me." I followed her down the long hall to another nurses' station. We passed the room where Stick was. The nurse was wiping the side of his face with a towel.

"Sit down here." She pointed at a low stool next to the desk. "Can you write?"

"Yes." I gritted my teeth as I sat down. The nurse pulled out a clipboard and slapped a pen on it.

"Fine. Fill this out." She thrust the board at me. I took it, but my fingers trembled as I lifted the pen. I tipped it against the page and started to write the date, but it came out a squiggly mess.

"I thought you said you could write."

I glared up at her. My jaw ached from holding my teeth together so hard. I tried to relax.

"I can. I will." I didn't like her breathing down my neck. Maybe I could fill out the form if she'd back off a bit.

"Give me that." She snatched back the pen and clipboard. I clasped my hands together to stop their trembling.

"Name?"

"Mine or his?"

She sighed. "His."

I looked toward the door of the room where the nurses

had taken Stick. "Steven Tyrone Childs." No one called him Stick but me.

The nurse wrote it down. "Age and birthday? His."

"Seventeen. October 8, 1950. Is he going to be all right?"

"I'm sure he'll be fine," she said, without looking up. "Parents' names?"

I took a deep breath. "Roland and Marjorie Childs."

The nurse raised her eyes to me as her pen slid through the letters. "Your father is Roland Childs?" I nodded. "Well," she said, looking back at the clipboard.

"I have to go to the bathroom," I said, standing up.

The nurse clicked the pen off. "It's down the hall. Go on, then." I walked away. Out of her sight, I stopped in the hallway beside the men's room door and closed my eyes.

"Sam!" Mama's voice called out. She rushed down the hall toward me, arms open to hug me.

I let her fold me against her. "I'm fine, Mama, I'm fine." She squished me to her and kissed my head, even though I was much too old to be fussed over. How had she found me so fast? I didn't even care—at least she was there.

"All right, baby. It's all right," she murmured. Father's heavy footsteps approached. I turned to face him.

"Father," I said, pulling away from Mama.

Father looked tall in the low-ceilinged hospital corridor. He pulled his hands out of his coat pockets and removed his gloves. "Where's your brother?" he asked, looking me in the eyes.

I was in trouble.

"They took him in there," I stammered, and pointed to the room where Stick was.

Father nodded. "Look at me. Are you hurt?" he asked.

"No, sir."

His gaze was piercing. He was trying to get the truth out of me. After a moment, his eyes softened and he patted me on the shoulder. "All right then. Let me see about your brother." He strode away and entered Stick's room.

A moment later, the nurse emerged. "I'll get the doctor now," she said. Mama and I followed Father into the room.

Stick lay in the bed, propped up against pillows. He had a thick white gauze pad taped to the side of his head. "I did what I had to do," he was saying. Father stood at the far side of the bed, near the window, looking out.

"You let your temper go," Father said. "We've talked about this."

"Father, I—"

"No." Father turned from the window. "When I went to work with Martin, I took an oath of nonviolence. I've upheld it to this day, and I expect you to do the same. No excuses. Is that understood?"

Stick sat up in the bed. "This wasn't some taunts at a

lunch counter! This wasn't ketchup on their heads! Look at my face! I'm not supposed to fight back to that?"

Father didn't always need words to make his point. He could have been a preacher—his eyes were like a sermon in and of themselves. Anyway, Stick knew as well as I did that some of the college kids who'd staged sit-ins to protest segregated lunch counters in the south had been beaten in addition to having condiments poured over their heads. They'd never fought back.

Today, we had.

Father and Stick stared at each other for a long while. Neither of them spoke.

"I'm going to find the doctor," Father said finally. His coattails flapped against my shins as he swept past me and out the door.

Stick flopped back against the pillows. Mama stroked his hair. Stick looked past her to me. "What'd you tell him?" he demanded.

I shook my head. "Nothing."

"We saw," Mama said, touching the edge of Stick's bandage. "From the podium, we saw."

Stick pushed her fingers away. "I'm not sorry I went after them," he muttered. "They were beating on innocent people. That old woman." He closed his eyes and pressed his head deeper into the pillow. "How can he ask me to just stand by and watch it happen?"

"Turn the other cheek," Mama said softly. She ate up Father's words like candy, without question.

I had questions, like Stick. I just didn't know how to ask them.

Father, Mama, and I sat in the waiting room for hours. At some point, Ty and Jerry came and sat with us. I tried not to look at Father, but he was watching me. All my life he'd talked a lot about actions and consequences. I couldn't even imagine what he thought I deserved for leaving a demonstration without permission. The very fact that he hadn't said anything to me for several hours was a bad sign.

People came and went from the waiting room. Every once in a while, Father approached the nurses at the desk to ask about Stick. At first, they told him the doctors were busy with other patients and they'd be right with us, but eventually, it got so they saw him coming and got real busy real fast. What was so hard about stitching up someone's head?

I got up.

"Where are you going?" Mama said.

"Bathroom," I said, but I didn't really have a destination in mind.

I walked past the nurses' desk and down the long hallway.

I strolled into the hospital gift shop. The man behind the cash register glanced up from his book and eyed me as I entered. I walked by a wall of get-well cards and a bunch of little baskets with IT'S A BOY and THINKING OF YOU balloons tied to them, then squeezed the foot of a bear with a heart sewn into its chest.

I stopped in front of a basket of fuzzy knit hats and mittens. The mittens made me think of Maxie Brown, the girl I might someday ask to be my girlfriend. If I could ever get her to say more than five words to me at a time. I thought of her standing in the schoolyard, her cold, bare hands balled up in fists at the ends of her sleeves. The sign on the basket read: MITTENS $2.50. HATS $4.00.

I stuck my hand in my pocket. I had a couple dollars on me, but I wasn't sure it would be enough.

"Put it back." The voice startled me, and I turned. The old man behind the counter glared at me.

"What?" I said.

"I said, put it back." He moved out from behind the counter and approached me, shaking his fist.

"Put what back?"

"Don't give me sass, boy. You think I can't see?" He came up and grabbed my wrist, yanking my hand out of my pocket. Two dollar bills and some coins dropped onto the floor as he pried open my fingers.

"I don't understand," I said. I glanced over his shoulder at the door. "I didn't take anything."

"Turn out your pockets, both of them." I inverted the linings in my other pocket. The man frowned.

"All right, now, get your sticky fingers out of my shop, you little"—he called me a couple of names that would have had Stick tossing fists, or made Father turn cool and stoic as he walked away—"Get out before I call the police." I stood there and took it.

I stared at my two dollars and change spread on the floor beside me, then at the purple mittens. Father would say, pick up your money, walk out right now, don't give this man the satisfaction of humiliating you, and take your business elsewhere. Stick would say, if you want the mittens, don't let this racist jerk stop you from getting what you want.

I bent over and gathered up the spilled cash. I took a deep breath as I straightened out. "I want to buy those mittens. The purple pair." I pointed.

The man stood there sizing me up. I waited. I'd have to brush past him to get out of the shop, and I didn't want to get that close. The man picked up the purple mittens and pointed in the direction of the register. He made me walk in front of him until we got to the counter. He moved around behind it, keeping an eye on me all the while. He shoved the mittens into a small paper sack and placed it on the counter.

"Two fifty," he said. I handed him my two dollars and counted out fifty cents. He recounted it twice, then pointed to the door. "Now get your thieving behind out of my shop, and don't come back here."

I reached for the bag and cleared my throat. "Can I have the receipt?" I said. No way I'd let him accuse me when I walked out.

The man ripped the little piece of paper clear of the register without moving his eyes from me and I watched him tuck it into the bag. I swallowed the automatic "thank you" that formed in my throat and left the shop without another word.

In the hallway, I leaned against the wall until my heart stopped racing. I tried to breathe away the tightness in my stomach, but it was stuck there, like someone's fist. I'd forgotten what happens when you go someplace new. How careful you had to be. Why I wasn't allowed to go into the white neighborhoods without Father or Mama.

I was still shaking a little as I made my way back to the waiting room. Father leaned forward in his seat when he spotted me. "Sam?" He looked concerned. "You all right?"

"Fine." I took my seat across from him. He watched as I folded down the top edge of the gift shop bag and placed it in my lap. I was sure he could see my hands trembling, that he could read what had happened by looking at my face.

But he didn't say anything more. He sat back, stroking his cheek with his fingertips and watching me with one of his thinking stares.

It was well after dark before they released Stick and all of us emerged from the hospital. At the curb, Jerry sat behind the wheel of our waiting car. Ty rushed toward us. Why?

A flashbulb exploded in my face. I threw up my arms. Questions burst like fireworks around us.

"Mr. Childs, who do you believe is responsible for your son's injury?"

"Will you try to find the men who attacked Steven and Sam?"

"Can you comment on your plans to respond to the incident?"

"Sam, Steve, what really happened out there?" One of the reporters leaned in close as he spoke. I could feel his breath on my cheek. My head filled with the sound of his camera *snap-snap-snapping*. Each flash blazed against my eyelids. Behind my closed eyes, the gift shop man's blunt fingers pointed, accusing me of being black. The man with the bottle still loomed in my mind, his sneer as sharp as the glass edges that had glinted in the sun.

Ty stepped between the reporter and me, steering me

toward the car. I tumbled into the backseat, right after Stick. Mama climbed in next. She slammed the door and held her handbag over the window to block the photographs. Father stood outside, Ty next to him, long enough to make a statement to the hungry newsmen.

Jerry glanced back from the driver's seat, his expression tense. We didn't used to have security for the demonstrations—Father didn't like the way it looked, like maybe he was afraid. But lately, there had been letters. Phone calls. Threats, more of them and harsher than the usual. I scrunched deeper into my seat thinking about the calls, especially. How scary it could be to pick up the phone and just hear someone breathing at the other end. Scarier than if they said something mean, because at least then you knew what they were thinking. Last week, Mama told me I wasn't allowed to answer the phone anymore, even if I was home alone. Especially then. I shivered. Today, I was glad for Ty and Jerry.

When the media moment ended, Father and Ty piled in and Jerry drove off. Ty checked the rearview mirrors repeatedly, making sure we weren't being followed. Jerry's wide shoulders hunched forward to make room for Father, who was sitting between them. We rode in tense silence, unusual for us. Ty was the friendly, chatty sort, even when he was working; not to mention Mama, who could carry on

keklamagoon

a conversation with the car itself if she felt like it. But she sat quietly, balancing her handbag on her knees. Stick and I were in big-time trouble if not even Mama could think of anything to say.

None of the newspeople followed us. As we rounded the corner onto our street, I let out a huge breath. Home. Just seeing the house drew some tension out of me, though the windows were dark, the curtains drawn as if no one had been around for a while. In the deep evening shadows the siding paint looked gray instead of cream. Our plan to come home early had backfired completely.

We said good night to Ty and Jerry in our driveway. As we walked up the path to the porch, I had an odd urge to climb onto the long slope of the roof and lie there, alone and away from everything.

"Samuel, go to your room," Father instructed as soon as we got inside. "Steven, couch."

"Yes, sir," I mumbled. I shuffled to the bedroom I shared with Stick and closed the door. Ten loose wooden building blocks lay scattered across my desk. I scooped them all up. It was definitely a ten-block kind of day. Breathing deeply, I forced myself to relax and steady my hand. Then I approached our castle.

The block castle towered over the foot of my bed, stretching so tall, it nearly touched the ceiling and so wide, we could only partly open my half of the closet door. I cradled the blocks in my left arm, picking up one at a time to place it. One, at the base by the main entrance annex. Two, at eye level, completing the royal arch. Three, right at the corner by the bed, sticking off like a gargoyle. Four.

I used to build for fun, for the sheer pleasure of crafting a miniature warehouse, office, palace, stable, restaurant out of rubble.

Five.

Lately, it was more like a way to leave the real world for someplace better. Just for a minute, I could focus only on the tower, only on the placement of each block.

Six. Seven.

As I reached above my head to set a block near the apex, I had to take such care not to knock any walls over that there wasn't room for anything else in my head, no space to even breathe.

Eight. Nine.

From the living room, the sounds alternated between Father's low rumbling tone and Stick's occasional grunting response. I could hear Father speaking, but I couldn't make out the words. He never raised his voice, no matter how mad he got.

Ten. I held the last block, thinking of where to put it. The perfectly edged rectangle felt good in my hand. Familiar and solid, almost big enough to cover my palm. We had some blocks that were cubes, and a few triangles for decoration, but mostly it was this kind. I bounced it on my fingers. Maybe I would save it for Stick.

I flopped onto my bed and closed my eyes, imagining the world inside our castle.

Stick and I used to lie on our beds after lights-out and play the game together, making up elaborate lives and characters, before we got too old to make-believe. My wall was covered with photos of famous buildings—the Wrigley Building, Marina City, the Egyptian pyramids, the Guggenheim Museum, the Taj Mahal, the palace of Versailles. The block tower could be any or all of them, and we had invented stories about the worlds that might exist inside each of their walls.

Stick pretended not to be as into it as I was, but he went along, adding pieces to the tower here and there when he felt like it. Anyway, he was the reason we still had the thing.

We'd started it when I was nine. I wanted to build a really big castle. Stick said okay, and we spent an entire day setting up an elaborate floor plan and building the base and everything. By the time we used every last block we had in the house, we had only built up a few inches from the ground.

"Let's build something else," I'd said, ready to tear down the walls and start over on something more manageable.

"No way," Stick had said.

"But we can't finish it," I said.

"Sure we can, we just need more blocks."

"From where?"

"I don't know. We'll get some."

"That'll take forever." I started to break apart the blocks, but Stick dragged me away, pulling me over by his bed.

"It'll be worth it," he insisted. I didn't understand what he meant.

"Come on, let's go outside," he'd said. So we went to play in the yard, and later whenever I mentioned tearing it down, Stick would say, "We're keeping it."

Stick was always like that—stubborn and patient. A lot of things ended up going his way because I'd get bored with the fight and give in.

I opened my eyes and studied the tower, admiring the way it loomed over my bed. Stick had been right back then. It was the neatest project we'd ever worked on. Definitely worth it.

Stick entered the room, slamming the door behind him. Frames banged against the wall. Stick's waterfall poster trembled, making it look like the water was actively pounding the rocks. The block tower, too, seemed to leap in surprise.

Stick yanked open the closet door, his elbow jabbing near the tower.

"Watch it!"

"Oh, now he doesn't want it to fall," Stick muttered. I slipped the last block under my pillow. Apparently he wasn't in the mood.

"How bad was it?" I asked. Stick shot me a look that made me want to crawl under the bed. "What did he say?"

Stick shook his head slightly but didn't answer.

"So, it's my turn now?" If I'd managed to forget reality for a second, I was fully back now.

Stick threw himself down on his bed. "No. You're off the hook."

"Yeah, right." I dragged myself up and trudged toward the door.

"Sam. You don't have to go out there."

I turned around. Stick lay across his bed, eyes closed, arms above his head. The gauze covering his forehead had come a little loose. I could see the stitched black knots underneath, holding his cut together.

"For real?" I couldn't tell if he was messing with me. I sat back down on the bed.

"Don't worry about it. He thinks it was all my idea," Stick said. "You're still his good little boy."

I laced my fingers together. "Didn't you tell him?"

"No reason to. It's covered. He expects this from me."

I got up. "I'm going to tell him it was my idea." Stick always stood up for me, tried to keep things from me, but I could be brave too.

"Sam, don't be stupid. It won't stop him from being mad at me. We'd just both be in trouble, is all."

"I can handle it." I wasn't sure I could, but Stick didn't have to know that.

"He wouldn't believe you, anyway."

"Stick—"

"Shut up, already! My head is killing me," he snapped.

Stick turned over, facing away from me, and lay in his bed without moving. It was too early to sleep, but I threw on some pajamas and climbed into bed. If he didn't want to talk to me, I didn't want to talk to him.

I had fallen into a calm and fuzzy place, almost asleep, when I heard muffled sniffing sounds coming from Stick's side of the room. I woke up instantly, alarmed. Stick never cried.

"I can't take it anymore," he whispered.

I didn't know what to say. I wasn't sure he was even talking to me. So I lay still, in the dark.

CHAPTER 2

SUNDAY MORNING, IT SNOWED. THICK FAT flakes, the kind you could catch on your tongue. Stick had the curtain pulled back with two fingers. He sat on the edge of his bed, all dressed and ready, staring into the white sky.

"I messed it up again," I said, fumbling with my tie. I'd wrapped and tucked it over and over, but the skinny part kept sticking out the bottom. I gave up, letting the ends hang down my chest. "I could tie my old tie," I muttered. I'd gotten a new one from Mama for Christmas. Stick kept saying the tie just wasn't broken in yet.

"How's your head?" I asked, sitting down to lace up my shoes. Stick touched his fingers to his temple, but didn't answer.

"Breakfast, boys!" Mama called. Stick let the curtain drop back into place and walked past me out of the room. I shuffled after him, wrestling with my tie.

Mama had a stack of waffles waiting on the table when Stick and I slid into our places. Father was flipping through the Sunday paper. When Stick sat down, Father laid the front page across his plate. Stick blinked, then looked back up at Father. I craned my neck to see across the table, but I couldn't read anything. I stood up for a better angle.

The story on the front page wasn't coverage of the demonstration. It was us. A picture of Stick and me leaving the hospital, his head all bandaged and me looking spooked as all get out. CHILDS'S SONS BEATEN AT PROTEST, the caption read. I sucked in my breath.

Mama walked in from the kitchen with a bowl of warm syrup and set it on the table. She took one look at the three of us and started rubbing the back of her hand against her forehead.

"Eat up, you two. We're going to be late for church," she said. When neither of us moved, Mama sighed. She pushed aside the paper, then forked two waffles onto each of our plates and spooned syrup over them. "Come on, now." She walked to the living room window, murmuring about how this might be the last good snowfall for the winter and we'd better enjoy it while it lasted.

I dug into the food because I was starving. We'd skipped dinner, but I hadn't realized it until right then. Stick sat there, looking at his food.

"Are you going to eat?" Mama asked him. He shook his head. I grabbed the waffles off his plate and put them away in a hurry, before Stick could change his mind.

Church was extra crowded. We sat all pressed together in the pew, with me wedged between Father and Stick. Neither of them had said a word all morning. I hadn't said anything either. Mama kept chatting us up, trying to get some conversation going. But we were wearing down her tongue.

We sat in our usual place, in the center section, fourth row from the front. Close enough, I supposed, so that God would definitely know we were there, but not so close that we appeared to be hogging too much of the Holy Spirit.

The choir filed into their two special rows behind the pulpit, gold robes rustling reverently against the dark wood pews. They had the best spot in the house; warm sunlight streamed over them through the stained-glass windows on either side of the altar. I lamented for the hundredth time the impossibility of creating stained-glass windows with blocks. That was one thing the castle was missing.

The pipe organ wheezed out the opening notes of a familiar tune. I lifted the worn hymnal and smoothed my fingers over the pages as I flipped through them. My voice was low, since I wasn't a good singer. Stick had a better voice, but he didn't join in, and I felt more alone than ever.

> *Some times I feel discouraged,*
> *And think my work's in vain,*
> *But then the Holy Spirit*
> *revives my soul again.*
> *There is a balm in Gilead*
> *To make the wounded whole;*
> *There is a balm in Gilead*
> *To heal the sin-sick soul.*

Stick stared straight ahead. I watched the row of neat black stitches across his temple. They moved up and down slightly as Stick clenched and unclenched his jaw. I wondered if it hurt.

Father's voice was strong as the congregation moved on to the second verse. I snuck a glance at him. His eyes were closed, his fingers wrapped around Mama's hand, stroking her knuckles with his thumb. The song made sense for me, and for Stick. Maybe even for Mama, but not Father. I never knew him to be discouraged.

It was a miracle Stick and I survived the fellowship hour. It got plain annoying. Everyone flocked around us, patting and poking me and reaching for Stick's bandage as if they could heal him with a touch. I smiled real big and did the best I could to keep them at bay, but Stick grunted only the minimum response, just enough interaction to keep Father satisfied.

I was used to crowds, to attention, but Stick and I usually tackled the mobs together. He would be real charming, and all the old church people loved him. My job was to stand there, shake hands, and throw out yeses and noes as needed.

When we finally escaped to the parking lot, I was bursting with frustration.

"Thanks a lot," I said.

"For what?"

"All your help back there with the old-goat patrol." That was our secret name for the old ladies who had their noses so far up everybody's business that they couldn't smell anything but gossip. They would quote the Bible like regular people toss out song lyrics. To hear them tell it, they were right there when Moses came down off the mountain. Some of them looked old enough too.

"You didn't say two words to anyone," I said. "Those guys knock all the brains out of your skull yesterday, or what?"

"Shut up." Stick hauled off and hit me. Not pretend, either. It actually hurt a little.

I rubbed my shoulder where the punch had landed. "Hey. What's wrong with you, anyway?"

"Leave me alone."

"Snap out of it, would you?"

"I said, shut up, before I hit you again." As he spoke, Father emerged from the front of the church. Mama was close behind him.

I grinned. "You gonna hit me while *he's* watching?" Stick glared at me as he crossed to the other side of the car and got in.

I thought Father was going to make us do a lot of chores or something to make up for yesterday, but the atmosphere in the house was punishment enough. Stick and I sat at the dining table after dinner doing our homework. Father worked at his desk in the living room, keeping his head down. He cleared his throat and sighed from time to time, the cold waves of his disappointment washing over us even from that distance. Mama puttered around doing whatever she usually did on Sundays: preparing her lesson plans, ironing a few shirts, running lots of water in the bathroom for some reason. She came out looking a little red-eyed. Still, she was the only one of us acting normal.

Then the phone rang. My whole body tensed. It rang

again. All of us fell into a state of suspended anticipation, a slow-motion moment. On the third ring, Mama lifted the receiver off the dining room wall.

"Hello? Oh, Coretta, hello." She turned her back on Stick and me, facing the living room. Father finally looked our way, though the expression on his face made me wish he hadn't.

"Yes, they're both fine," Mama said. "I'm surprised the news traveled all the way to Atlanta."

Stick and I exchanged a glance at this unexpected twist—Dr. King's wife calling to see if we were okay. It never occurred to me that Dr. King himself might find out what we had done. Judging by the frown on Stick's face, he hadn't thought of that either.

"Yes. Yes, I know," Mama said. "I thank God every day that they come home."

No one seemed to realize we'd fought. We were victims, in the world's eyes. But not in Father's. I couldn't bear to look at him.

Though he never said it, Father was always worried about disappointing Dr. King and the others, disappointing the movement. I supposed it must be hard being famous, the way people look too closely at everything you do. The way you can never stray too far from the thing you're famous for without the world getting up in your business.

It was that way for me at school sometimes, like when Father was arrested a few years ago. Or like last year when Dr. King spent a few months in town "stirring up trouble," as the white folks liked to say. Since it was me in trouble this time, not Father, it could be worse than even last year was. I dreaded going to school the next day.

"Well, we'd love to have him visit Chicago again," Mama was saying. "There's always a place at our table."

I got a weird feeling when she said that, like it was just yesterday Dr. King had been over for dinner. I'd come home from school in a grumbly mood, what with all the comments I'd been dealing with at school. Father and Dr. King had been doing a lot of work in the projects, housing work. Every day, I heard about it—not because people were unhappy that he was here, but because the police presence in the neighborhoods they were working in was extreme.

"Come in here and rinse these greens," Mama had called the instant I came in the door. "We're having company tonight."

"What company?" I grumbled, entering the kitchen. "Do we have to?"

"Dr. King, for one," she said, then proceeded to list a few other friends of Father's.

"Really?" It had been a very long time since I'd seen Dr.

King up close and in person, though Father got together with him often. Sometimes they traveled together.

I washed my hands and started rinsing dirt off the leaves. I surveyed the meat, vegetables, and dough Mama had set out on the counter. "We're feeding Dr. King pot pie and collard greens?"

"Martin's been on the road for six months, baby. Even famous preachers need a good home-cooked meal from time to time." She spread a circle of dough over the pan, pressing the edges into place. She peered at me out the corner of her eye. "Anyway, are you saying my pot pie's not good enough for Dr. King?"

"Your pie's the best, Mama."

"That's what I thought you said. Hmm. I put my foot in that pot pie."

I wrinkled my nose as dramatically as possible. "Smells great, Mama."

She'd laughed. "It doesn't smell at all yet; it's not cooked." She'd squeezed my nose between two knuckles. "But you get points for working your way onto my good side."

One thing was certain: I wouldn't be getting points for anything today.

Mama shifted from one foot to the other, her back still to us. "Yes, Coretta, please do send him our best. All right. Take care. Good-bye." She hung up the phone, then retreated to the bedroom without acknowledging any of us.

I wished she would have said something, I didn't know what. Anything might have made me feel better.

Father turned back to his work. Stick let his head drop in his hands. His posture echoed the way I felt. Few things were as bad as disappointing Father or Mama, but knowing that Dr. King might find out we'd messed up was one of them.

I remembered feeling this exact way last year, the same night Dr. King came over for dinner. I'd barely thought about that night since then, but I recalled this feeling. Like we'd crossed a line without even meaning to.

That night, Stick and I had gone to our room after the meal, where we were supposed to do our homework. We did, but we also cracked the door so we could listen a bit to the meeting going on in the living room.

Sometime after dark, the window rattled, and we both looked over. Stick's friend, Bucky Willis, waved from outside, motioning for us to open the window. His breath fogged the glass.

Stick leaned over and popped the lock, lifting the sash. No sooner had the glass cleared his forehead than Bucky practically dove into the house, landing with a thud in the middle of our floor.

"Hello, boys."

"Shhh!" Stick and I exclaimed in unison, creating a sound altogether louder than Bucky's entrance had been. I leaped to the door, pushing it closed. Stick shut the window quickly before too much cold air came in.

Bucky's eyes rounded beneath the slight brim of his afro. "What's up?" he whispered. He shook his shoulders out of his too-thin winter coat and blew on his fingers.

"What are you doing here?" Stick asked. He glanced at me as he spoke. We both knew why Bucky had come. Ever since his family lost their apartment, Bucky'd been living on the street. He often snuck in after bedtime to crash on our floor, especially now that it was full-on winter.

Footsteps in the hall. Father. Stick shoved Bucky's shoulder. "Get in the closet. In the closet—now," he whispered. Bucky did, easing the door shut behind him as Stick and I assumed studious postures on our beds.

Father knocked and opened the door. "Everything all right?" he asked, surveying the room.

"We're fine," Stick said. He had long since perfected the innocent look. I, on the other hand, kept my head bowed over my history textbook. My inability to bluff had cost us smaller battles than this one.

"We heard a noise." Father went to the window and peered out, his jaw tense. "Did you hear it?"

"I, uh, threw a book at Sam," Stick said, sounding appropriately guilty but contrite. I didn't know how he managed it. "It was kinda loud when it fell, I guess."

"It kinda hurt, too," I mumbled, trying to do my part.

Father moved back to the doorway, resting his hand on the knob. "Well, some of the men stepped out to walk around the house, just in case."

That gave me chills. One time, someone had thrown a brick through our bedroom window in the middle of the night, and the living room windows, too. Anything that could happen to me and Stick, or to Father alone, could happen ten times over with Dr. King around.

I lowered my head again, suppressing the urge to tell Father that it was only Bucky. I'd tell him anything to smooth the worried crease from his brow. Father looked at each of us again, then closed the door.

Stick opened the closet door to release Bucky, who put on a mock pout. "You really know how to make a guy feel welcome. What was that about?" The silly expression morphed into genuine uncertainty. "I thought your father didn't mind me coming over. Is it cool, for real?"

Stick shook his head. "Yeah, but not now. We have special company tonight. Dr. King and some other folks."

"No kidding?" Bucky looked at me and smiled, exposing the prominent front teeth that had earned him his nickname. His real name was Clarence.

"Sure thing," I said. "We had dinner, and now they're meeting with Father."

"I can't believe he's in your house, man." Bucky shook his head. "Dr. King himself."

"He's supposed to be here. You're not." Stick jerked his head toward the window.

Bucky put his coat back on, then sighed. "I got nowhere for tonight, brother."

"You can come back later, when they're gone."

"You ain't gonna introduce me?" Bucky grinned, smoothing down his collar like he was prepping for a date.

"Get out," Stick said, not in a mean way. We didn't really want to send Bucky away, but we didn't want to get in trouble in front of Dr. King and everyone either.

"Sending me out into the cold," Bucky said with a sniff. "I understand. I do." He conjured up his best, most pathetic wounded-animal eyes.

Stick groaned and rolled back against his pillow. "Stay. But keep your big mouth shut."

Bucky's wide grin was like money falling from the sky—free, but you felt like you'd earned it.

"You ain't never heard a mouse as quiet as me." He shrugged out of his coat and resettled himself on the floor between our beds. "Yes, sir. You won't even know I'm here.

Not a whisper. Not a breath. Quiet like nothing. Quieter."

Stick pulled the pillow from under his head and chucked it to the floor. Bucky took it in the chin and shoulder. We all laughed.

"Shut up and read something, man. Under the bed." Stick motioned with his foot toward the scattering of books and magazines beneath his bed. Stick's half of the room was crowded with reading material; he read just about everything in sight.

Bucky nodded but reached for his own bag instead. "I brought something of my own to read."

Stick sat up. "Yeah?"

I turned from my pretend studying to look too. Reading was Bucky's least favorite pastime, mainly because he wasn't all that good at it. When he came over, Stick made him read magazines just to keep him quiet, but we both knew Bucky flipped through the pages studying the pictures and diagrams but ignoring the words altogether. He was smart, but not word-smart like Stick. He could fix anything that had moving parts—in fact, Father often said Bucky'd make a brilliant engineer if he'd settle down long enough to finish school. But he didn't have time for school anymore, not with his sister, Shenelle, and their mom to support. He worked long shifts each day at Roy Dack's auto shop, trying to save enough to get his family back into an apartment.

"Sure thing," Bucky said, extracting a newspaper from his bag. He displayed it proudly in front of him. "Have you seen this?"

Stick's expression hardened. "Yeah." He took the paper from Bucky and folded it up before I got a good look. "You can't read that here. Not now."

"Hey, I want to see." I moved up from the end of my bed, getting closer to Bucky. Stick frowned at me, then glared at Bucky.

"Another time," Stick said. He handed the paper back to Bucky. "Put it away."

I leaped off my bed and grabbed the newspaper out of Bucky's hand. Stick shot me a don't-you-dare look. I sent back a dirty look of my own. If something interesting was happening, I was not going to be left out. I unfolded the page. "*The Black Panther*," I read aloud. "'All power to the people.'"

"Sam." The single syllable sliced through the air. "Later." His tone was so sharp and thick with annoyance, maybe even anger, that I released the paper into his hands. He swatted Bucky on the side of the head with it.

"Dr. King is in our living room, and you want to sit here contemplating armed revolution? I don't think so."

Bucky held up his hands. "Whoa. Put away the big words, bro. I'm not trying to get militant. Not my style. But new things are happening out there. It's exciting."

"Out where?" I was confused.

"Oakland, in California," Stick said. "And people getting killed is not exciting." He dropped the paper in Bucky's lap. "It's not even new."

"No, man. That's not even what I'm talking about," Bucky said. "They've got these ideas about how things should be."

Stick lay back on his bed. "Well, we all have that, Buck. Really, we'll talk about it later."

Bucky opened the paper. "Right here"—he pointed— "it says they want everyone guaranteed a place to live, no matter what. I dig that." He spoke quieter than usual, keeping his head down. He moved his finger along the page. "And here, it says they want black people released from prison because the system is so messed up. Well, you know how I feel about that."

Stick and I fell into a respectful silence. Bucky's father was killed by prison guards a year or so earlier. He shouldn't have been in jail in the first place, but that was how it went.

Stick scribbled something in one of his notebooks and showed it to Bucky. Bucky folded the Panther newspaper and replaced it in his bag. He took a magazine from Stick's pile and reclined against the bed, flipping through it as casually as anything. I wondered what Stick had written that so completely silenced him. Bucky was a lot of things, but discreet was not one of them.

That was more than six months ago. I'd never heard either of them mention the paper again. In fact, I'd all but forgotten about it. I shifted in my seat, wishing I could forget it all again. I didn't like the feeling the memory inspired—the vague sense that the world around me was not as I believed it to be.

C H A P T E R 3

WAS RIGHT ABOUT ONE THING: CHURCH HAD BEEN
bad, but school was a whole other nightmare. Everyone
had seen my picture in the paper.

"Hey, Sam, you all right?" The sentiment echoed down
the school corridors. It got to the point where I couldn't tell
who was asking anymore. I could've had blood gushing out
of ten places and I think I would've said, "Yeah, fine."

Days like this gave me a glimpse of what it was like
to be popular, which usually I wasn't. Stick was the type
who gathered lots of friends and admirers, had girls coming
after him and all of that. I was the one in the shadows. Out
in the world, I was Roland's son. Here at school, Steve's
little brother. Listening to all the voices around me acting
concerned, I remembered that even though everyone knew
my name, no one really knew me. It was probably just as
well—I could never be as strong as Father or as smooth as
Stick.

Normally, I didn't mind the learning part of school as much as most people did, but that day, I considered skipping class. Everyone else did it from time to time, but not me. It wasn't the sort of thing I could get away with. Aside from the annoying fact that my parents could always sense when I disobeyed them, Mama actually worked in the office of my school, just two narrow desks away from the daily attendance rolls.

All day, I couldn't concentrate. My mind traveled in a hundred directions. Nobody called on me, so I felt free to zone out. During history, I looked out the third-floor classroom windows at the buildings in the neighborhood. This class faced away from the projects, out toward where I lived. The land sloped up into a slight hill, which was great for looking down on the houses. Several streets of row houses were closest to the school, then behind them the streets widened some and there were individual houses, like the kind we lived in. I noticed the way the roofs all sloped at the same angle on one street, then shifted to a different angle on the next. If I ever got to build houses, I wouldn't make them all the same in a line like that.

Father and Mama wanted me and Stick to go to college and everything. When I was little, I assumed that meant we were supposed to become lawyers, like Father. I could see Stick as a lawyer, making speeches like Father, or like the ones on TV who defend wrongfully accused people. But not me.

Once, I asked Father if he thought I'd make a good lawyer. He said I could be good at anything I put my mind to. I was in fifth grade at the time, and filled with an odd sense of bravery, so I told him I didn't want to go to college, I just wanted to build things. He said I didn't have to be a lawyer, I could be anything I wanted—that's what college was for. The next day, he brought me a book about famous buildings and the men who had designed and built them. That's when I decided that I wanted to be an architect.

I paid a little more attention in math, because it was one of the most important subjects for architects. Plus, it was a windowless classroom, so there wasn't much else to look at besides the chalkboard.

Sitting through class was rough, but the worst was when Maxie Brown passed me in the hall. She didn't even look over. I would have preferred being invisible to everyone else, but not to Maxie. Usually, we at least made eye contact.

After last bell, I hurried to my locker. The paper bag with the mittens was sitting on the shelf. I stared at it for a moment. Today was supposed to be the day I finally got through to her. That had been the plan, but now, it seemed dumb. I couldn't believe I'd even imagined that some stupid fuzzy mittens would get her to like me.

I closed my locker. Why make a bad day worse?

In the evening, Stick and I sat at the table doing our homework. I always did math first, because it was my best subject. Stick was a word man. He was busy scratching out some kind of essay.

Mama stood scrubbing dishes in the sink, singing to herself. Mama loved to sing, but she was always a little off-key when there wasn't any music going. She had her feet moving and her backside waving and suds splashed up along the side of the sink. She launched into some high, squeaky melody and Stick and I glanced at each other. I wrinkled my nose. He grunted and moved his pencil.

Father was sitting in his chair in the living room. He had some papers spread open on his knees, but he wasn't really working. His head was turned toward the kitchen door, and he was smiling a little. He caught me watching and cleared his throat.

"You done, Sam?"

"Not yet." I went back to my problem set.

Father stood and went into the kitchen. He came up behind Mama and grabbed her waist, dancing with her back. He dragged her from the sink, twirling her around the kitchen.

"Roland, my hands are wet," she cried. She tried to hide her smile. Stick and I both stopped working to watch them.

"I love a woman who sings while she works," Father said. He kissed her cheek. "I don't even care if it is off-key."

Mama beat on his chest, then pulled free, glaring at him. She moved back to the sink, turning around to toss Father a dry dishtowel. "I love a man who dries my dishes. Even if he does insult me."

Father laughed. He took the dishtowel and held it tight between his fists. He did a little footwork moving toward the counter.

"Let's hear some more sweet tunes." He leaned in to kiss Mama again, but she ducked away.

"Uh-unh. You want singing, call Diana Ross. Now, are you gonna stand there and dance or are you gonna help me with these dishes?"

Father began drying the plates. "You've got to watch what you say, because you know if that Diana Ross came knocking at the door calling my name, I might just have to go with her."

Mama whipped the dishcloth at him. Water splattered all over him and the dishes he'd just dried.

"Now you've gone and done it." Father frowned, mopping his face with the drying towel.

Mama pointed at the row of dishes. "You missed a spot."

Father looked up at the ceiling and started humming "Rescue me, and take me in your arms, rescue me."

Stick bent over his essay again, but I kept watching the two of them in the kitchen. Father was hardly ever so cheerful. I should have been more proud of him for being famous. But I wasn't. I wanted him like this. Dancing in the kitchen, with a smile on his face and no one's eyes on him but mine.

A loud knock at the door startled all four of us. Stick and I both jumped about a mile. Father and Mama looked at each other and burst out laughing.

Father tossed the dishtowel at Mama. "Diana, here I come," he said, rubbing his hands together.

Mama snatched the cloth out of the air and waved it at him. "You go on, now, I can't be bothered."

Father backed through the doorway, still humming.

"Who is it?" Mama called.

"Fred and Leon," Father said. As he opened the door, I saw Fred Wood and Leon Betterly standing on the porch.

Mama twisted the faucet so the water flowed more gently. Better for listening in, I supposed. Stick and I stood up to greet Father's best friends. They had been with him when he first went to march with Dr. King, and had walked beside him through everything—riots and marches, fire hoses and police dogs. He never had to ask—they were always there. I wondered if I would ever be strong enough to know how it felt to stand up.

"Steven. How's the head, son?" Fred bellowed at Stick.

Stick always touched his head when anyone mentioned it. "Hi, Mr. Wood. It's much better, sir, thank you," he said.

"Good to hear it." Fred was short and thin, but what he lacked in size he made up for in volume. Father never conferred with Fred in public—he didn't know how to whisper.

Father clapped Stick gently on the shoulder. "Why don't you boys finish up your work in your room." We gathered our books and went down the hall.

Once we were in our room, we did anything but study. We tossed a little plastic ball back and forth for a while, and I tried to think of a good way to ask Stick what I should do about Maxie.

"Hey, Stick, you know that girl I was telling you about?" I tried to sound casual.

Stick snorted. "Which? There've been so many."

I frowned. "No, there haven't." Stick laughed harder. He was messing with me. "Stick—"

"I know, I know. Maxie Brown. She's definitely got it."

"Got what?"

"What it takes. Pretty, smart, funny—all that stuff."

"You don't even know her. How do you know she's smart and funny?" She was both, of course. And pretty, too.

"Well, I figure you wouldn't fall for a girl without a brain in her. And she's got you running left and right chasing after her, so she must have a sense of humor." Stick grinned. I lobbed the ball hard at his head. He winced as he ducked out of the way.

"Well, so, I went to the gift shop yesterday," I began.

"Yeah, what was with that?" Stick said, the grin creeping back across his face. "I see you carrying a hospital gift shop bag around, and yet I get nothing." He held out his hands.

I laughed. "Not for you."

Stick scowled. "You go to the gift shop and you don't even bring back a gift for the poor, wounded patient. Your brother, I might add. And then you have the nerve to ask him for advice? Shoot, you'd better keep on walking."

My smile dropped as I remembered being in the gift shop. "For real, though," I said. "I don't know what to do." I told him about the mittens and my plan for Maxie, careful not to say too much about what had happened.

Stick sighed. "Look, you already bought the mittens. The worst that can happen is she'll dis you and still keep them. Best-case scenario, you get a kiss. Not a bad range of odds."

I nodded. I felt a little better about things, but the thought of walking up to Maxie always made my stomach flutter.

Stick breathed like he was about to speak, then he paused. "Also, you shouldn't avoid doing something worthwhile just because you're afraid of what might happen."

I nodded again, but somehow, I wasn't sure Stick was talking about me and Maxie anymore.

I walked out of school the next day, clutching the brown sack, and immediately scanned the schoolyard for Maxie. I spotted her on the front steps, and walked over. "Hi," I said.

"Hi." Maxie stood on the third step down, arms crossed. I took a moment to look at anything but her. The scarred brick face of the school, three floors and a thousand sad stories tall. The chain-link fence marking the playground edges. Funny how it had barbed wire at the top, as if anyone would try to get into school if they didn't have to be there.

"Can I—" My tongue got all tied up and I chickened out. I sighed. This was supposed to get easier. She knew it was coming, anyway. I asked the same question practically every day, and she always gave the same answer. Maxie stood there, waiting to complete my humiliation.

"Can I walk you home?" I said.

"I know my way home."

Sometimes I thought maybe she waited outside just to hear me ask so she could say no. Stick said girls played games like this all the time, and if you wanted to get anywhere you had to play along until you learned the rules.

"I know," I said. "Just for company, I meant."

Maxie raised her eyebrows. I held my breath. "Maybe tomorrow," she said quickly. She pulled her bare hands up inside the sleeves of her coat. "I gotta go." She started to walk away. I swallowed hard. Now or never.

"I got something for you," I said. The words came out mumbled like I was clearing my throat or something. She would never go for me.

"What did you say?" She turned back to me and wrinkled her forehead.

"This is for you," I said, holding out the paper bag.

"Yeah?" she said. "For me?" She stood there looking at me, looking at the bag.

I shifted my feet. "Yeah. I thought they were—nice. I mean, I knew you didn't have—I thought you'd like them." It was maybe thirty degrees outside, but I stood there sweating.

I shook the bag until she took it and peeked inside. The corners of her mouth shot up, and she gave me a bewildered, wide-eyed look.

Maxie slid her hands into the mittens. Then she smiled as big as I've ever seen her smile. "Thanks, Sam. What's it for?"

What's it for? "Uh, for you," I said. *So you'll let me walk you home.* "No reason."

Maxie grinned again. "Well, come on, then," she said. She skipped down the stairs and strode across the schoolyard. I stood stuck in place. I couldn't believe it. In the middle of the yard, she turned around. "Sam! Are you coming, or what?" she yelled.

I ran and caught up with her at the edge of the schoolyard. She snapped her fingers at me. Well, she tried, anyway. The mittens made it tricky, but I knew what she was doing, so I laughed.

"Gotta keep up, man," she said. She grinned. I grinned back. It didn't get any better than that.

We started toward her house. She walked fast for a girl, I thought. Like she had places to be and nothing could keep her from getting there. I liked that. I wanted to go places too.

She didn't say a word to me as we walked, but I was too happy to care. She looked up at me once, though, as we passed the last intersection before the long stretch of projects began.

I studied buildings a lot, partly to get ideas for the

block tower. It struck me odd, each time I thought about it, how buildings could have such personalities. The stores and apartments Maxie and I walked past had seen sad times, and looked as if they'd taken much of the sadness upon themselves. They reminded me of children lined up in an orphanage—seen but abandoned, together but alone. Unloved.

I almost reached for Maxie's hand right then, but I feared it was too much too soon. As we approached the corner of her street, she slowed. We turned onto her block, and she walked even slower. In front of her building she stopped altogether and turned to me. "Well, this is it," she said, staring at her toes.

"Okay," I said. I already knew where she lived, but I wasn't about to tell her that.

She raised her head and looked straight at me with a strange light in her eyes. "And?" she said, her tone daring me to comment.

I looked up at the building, at its eight rows of windows, like worried eyes gazing down upon the street. I shrugged. "And what?"

She blinked and smiled. "Never mind. Nothing." She shook her head. "Aren't you cold?" she asked.

"Nah, it's not so bad," I said, trying not to shiver. My face was freezing, but I didn't care. If Maxie wanted to stand out here and talk to me, I wasn't going to complain.

She nodded and tugged her hat down over her ears. She half smiled up at me. She was so cute, I had to look away so she wouldn't think I was some kind of freak, staring at her. She cupped her hands and blew into her new mittens.

"Warm," she said, flashing me that great half-smile again. "Feel." She put her hands on my cheeks. Warm was an understatement.

She pulled her hands away, and we stood there for a few minutes longer.

"So, I guess I'd better get going," I said finally.

"Yeah," she said. "See you." She went toward her building. At the door, she turned around and waved both hands at me. I smiled as I walked up the block.

I slowed when I saw Stick standing on the opposite corner, talking to a slick-looking brother in a black leather jacket and heavy combat boots. The brother was tall, had a three-inch crown of hair on top of him. He and Stick clasped hands, then pulled together and bumped shoulders. The brother leaned in the window of the car idling beside them, pulled out a small flat box, and handed it to Stick. He thumped Stick on the back, got in the car, and drove off.

Stick turned the box over in his hands, studying it closely. A moment later he raised his head and spotted me. He looked a little surprised, but nodded hello.

I crossed the street. "Who was that?"

"A friend," Stick said, looking after the car. We started walking toward home.

"What friend?"

Stick rubbed his hand over his neck and looked at me sideways. "What are you doing over here, anyway?"

I shrugged. "Just walking Maxie home."

"Yeah?" Stick gave me a sharp look out the corner of his eye. "She your girl now, or what?"

"Naw." I kicked the ground. "We're just friends."

"We're just friends," he mimicked. I slugged him in the arm. He staggered to the side, laughing.

"Shoot, that was weak," he hooted, jogging a circle around me.

"C'mon back, I'll get you good," I threatened, smacking my fist into my other palm.

Stick grinned. He knew I was bluffing. I didn't feel like fighting him. I was still thinking about Maxie.

Stick moved back around beside me. I caught a glimpse of something in his hand.

"What did he give you?" I asked.

Stick cleared his throat. "Loaned me a book," he said. He lifted it so I could see, then lowered it fast. I couldn't read the title.

I stuck my hand out. "Can I see?"

"Maybe later," Stick said. He blinked a lot, which meant he was lying. Stick usually told me most everything I wanted to know. When he got secretive like this, it meant something bad. I shivered. Stick could keep his secret. I didn't want it.

CHAPTER 4

A FEW DAYS LATER, I MET MAXIE ON THE corner of her street at six thirty in the morning. We walked in silence toward the school. Maxie tucked her chin into the thin collar of her coat. She had her hands in her pockets, but the edges of the purple mittens poked out around her wrists. On the way home today, I would hold her hand. Maxie glanced up and caught me looking. I stuck my hands in my pockets. Maybe tomorrow.

"So, why'd you want to meet me so early?" I asked.

Maxie skipped a few steps ahead of me, then turned around and walked backward so we were looking at each other. "For breakfast."

I only had fifty cents in my pocket. "What are we eating?"

"Whatever they're serving."

"Where?"

"At school. You know, The Breakfast." She spoke like it was in caps: The Breakfast.

"I've never been." I kept walking, Maxie in front of me. Garbage bags lined the curb waiting for collection and the concrete was uneven in places, but she moved right down the center of the sidewalk, never taking her eyes off me.

"Never?" Maxie stared at me. "It's free, you know."

"I know," I said, as if I knew. "Turn left." Maxie spun around front and we turned into the schoolyard. Rows of tables lined the pavement and dozens of children had gathered to eat breakfast. Four guys stood behind a folding table beneath the basketball hoops, dishing up oatmeal to kids crowded around them. Stick was one of the servers.

"No way."

Maxie twirled in front of me. "I said they're giving out breakfast. You didn't believe me?"

"I believed you," I said. "I don't believe that." I pointed at Stick.

"What?"

"That's my brother."

Maxie studied the four guys behind the serving table. "Which one?"

"On the left."

"Steven's your brother?"

"You know him?"

Maxie stared at me like I had two heads. "Yeah, he's here about every day. That's my brother next to him, Raheem. Anyway, Steve's cool. Not as intense as some of the other guys from the Party."

"What party?"

"The Black Panthers," Maxie said. "They look out for us, you know? Hey, how come you don't know about them, your brother being a member and all?"

I shrugged. "He does his thing, I do mine." I tried to brush it off, but the Black Panthers? If Stick had joined, why hadn't he told me about it?

"I thought that was just out in California," I said. "It's here now?" I didn't completely know what "it" was, but I was sure going to find out now. I tried to recall what all Bucky and Stick had said about them the night Bucky'd brought the paper over.

"Not officially. But it will be."

Maxie and I got in line for oatmeal. We pressed forward with the other kids until we got to the front of the line. Stick grabbed a bowl from the stack and looked up. He froze mid-scoop, a big glob of oatmeal stuck to his spoon, suspended over the dish.

"Don't stop on my account," I said. "That stuff's not going to serve itself." As if to prove me wrong, the scoop of cereal slid right off the spoon and dropped into the bowl as I spoke. Maxie laughed, grabbing the bowl away from Stick.

"Nice," she said, but I couldn't join her laughing. Stick had my attention. His closed expression told me I had walked in on something I wasn't supposed to see. He stood still, spoon in the air, looking as if he was deciding whether to get mad or to ignore me. Then he spooned me a bowl, and Maxie and I went to sit down.

Bucky Willis sat at the end of one of the long tables. "Let's go over there," I said.

Maxie nodded. "Sure."

Bucky bent over his bowl, spooning down oatmeal faster than I've ever seen anyone eat.

"Hey, Buck."

He glanced up. "Sam, my man, what's cookin'?" Bucky grinned his famous grin.

"Just the usual," I said, sitting down beside him. My back was to Stick, which was how I wanted it. This morning was supposed to be for Maxie and me. "This is Maxie."

Bucky nodded. "I know Maxie. How's it goin', girl?"

"It's going." Maxie sat across from us.

Bucky scraped up the last of his oatmeal and glanced at the food line. "They have a lot left when you were up there?"

"Looked like there was plenty to me," I said.

"Perfect." Bucky stood up. "Back in a few."

He got back in line. "I haven't seen Bucky in a while," I said. Stick used to bring him by the house all the time, but lately, Stick hadn't been home much himself.

"He's around," Maxie said. "Working in Roy Dack's auto shop."

"He's doing okay?"

Maxie stirred her cereal for a moment. "He gets by. They got the apartment back, at least."

"Yeah." Bucky's job paid the bills now, so he'd probably never come back to school.

"He takes good care of his mom and Shenelle, though." Maxie nodded toward Bucky's little sister, running in the schoolyard with her friends, her red-ribboned pigtails bouncing behind her.

Bucky returned with a second heaping bowl of oatmeal. He waved his spoon at Maxie's and my bowls, which were still full.

"Y'all better eat up, 'cause in a minute, I'll be looking for thirds." He grinned. You couldn't help but smile back. Even with all the things he had going on, Bucky was never anything but cheerful. No wonder everybody liked him.

Maxie's brother came up beside us. She made a face at him.

"Hi, Raheem," Bucky said.

"Hey," I said.

Raheem towered over the table, a bowl of oatmeal in his hand. He seemed about seven feet tall. "Hi, Buck," he said, then turned to me. "Hey, man. Haven't seen you around here."

"First time."

"This is Steve's brother, Sam," Maxie said.

"Good to meet you." Raheem and I clasped hands. "Maxie doesn't bring a lot of guys around, you know." He pointed a long, stern finger at me. "You treat her right."

"What do you want, Heem?" Maxie snapped. She stabbed her spoon into her oatmeal and shot him a dirty look. Even that, on her, was cute.

Raheem grinned. "Wednesdays, six thirty," he said, clamping a hand on my shoulder. "You ought to come down, check out the political education classes, my man. They talk up some serious stuff in there, you hear what I'm saying?"

"Yeah, sure," I said. "I'll check it out." I wanted to ask him more about the Panthers, but I didn't want to look dumb in front of Maxie.

"See you around." Raheem nodded to Maxie, then ambled off. Maxie kicked me under the table and winked. I kicked her back. We pressed the toes of our shoes against each other. It wasn't holding hands, but it was something.

o   o   o

Maxie met me on the steps after school. She led the way toward her house. I held back a smile as she turned down a street that took us a little out of the way. If I just reached out and took her hand, what would happen? Between her mittens and my gloves, we wouldn't really even be touching. It'd be like a practice. I flexed my fingers over and over, getting ready.

As we neared Bryant Street, where Maxie lived, I still hadn't made my move. I'd have to wait until tomorrow, because it was looking too late for today.

Music blared from a radio perched atop a phone booth down the block, where a group of men leaned against cars parked in front of the barbershop. Bucky came hurrying down the street past them. He waved and crossed toward us. "Hey, Sam. Maxie."

"Hey, Bucky. You finally got a free afternoon?" Maxie said.

"No, girl, I'm on the clock right now. Just dropping off some parts to a guy up the block." He pointed with his thumb over his shoulder. His hands were smudged with dirt and grease.

"I'm glad I ran into you, Sam," he went on. "Do me a favor, will ya? Tell Steve to stop by the shop tomorrow. We gotta talk. It's real important. I tried to catch him earlier, but I missed my shot."

"Yeah, no problem, Bucky. I'll tell him."

"Thanks, man, I gotta go. Get back to work 'fore they dock me." Bucky grinned and slapped my shoulder. "Catch ya later." He jogged off down the sidewalk, then slowed to wave at three guys coming out of the mini grocery across the street carrying bottles of soda. One of them called out to him, and Bucky turned partway around, still jogging.

"You coming tonight, man?"

"Can't. Working," Bucky called back. He waved again as he dashed toward the corner.

Two policemen stepped around the corner, right in front of Bucky. I jerked my head toward them. Maxie gasped.

Bucky was looking back over his shoulder, but still running forward. The two officers ambled around the corner, probably making their regular rounds through the neighborhood. Bucky rammed into the police officers, barreled right smack between them.

Bucky turned around, flustered. "Excuse me, Officers. I didn't see you." He started to move on, but one of them held up his hand.

"Not so fast, buster. What are you running from?"

"Nothing. I'm going to work." Bucky smiled.

"Put your teeth back in your head, boy, 'fore I knock 'em out," the stockier cop said. His stomach jiggled over his gun belt as he and his partner laughed.

Bucky swallowed hard. "I'm on my way back to my job." Again he tried to move away from them. This time, the taller cop drew his nightstick and laid it across Bucky's chest.

"Hold on just a minute, pal. We'll see about that. Where do you work?"

"What do you want to know that for? I didn't do nothing."

The tall cop looked Bucky over. "Do nothing sounds about right. Now, you want to tell us about this job of yours?"

Bucky balled his hands into fists, but nodded politely. "I fix cars."

"What's your name?"

Bucky stood without speaking. My heart pounded. He couldn't tell them his name. The stocky cop drew his nightstick and jammed the tip into Bucky's stomach. "I'm not going to ask again."

Bucky straightened up and shook his head slightly. The officer slammed the baton into Bucky's stomach again. Bucky doubled over from the force of the blow, pressing his arms against his stomach. The hit echoed in my gut—along with the horrible knowledge that everything was about to get worse.

The second cop's baton caught Bucky on the chin and

jerked him back up. Everyone on the street turned to look. The cops took turns striking Bucky with their nightsticks, fists, and feet. The radio in the background seemed to sing louder, the cheerful pop tune warring with the sick *thwack* of baton blows against skin.

The tall cop bent close to Bucky, his square nose practically touching Bucky's cheek, and said something. Bucky reacted sharply, jerking backward, his fists stretched out in front of him. The cop laughed and hammered Bucky's arms with his baton.

The music cut suddenly and the silence suffocated the street. The air grew thick, hard to breathe without choking. Only the hum of cars on nearby streets disturbed the still air. The stocky cop lifted the radio from his belt and spoke into it.

Maxie moved closer to me. This couldn't be happening right in front of us, especially not to Bucky. It went on forever. Finally the tall cop brought his nightstick down hard against Bucky's temple. The blow connected, making a loud *crack*. Maxie turned her face into my shoulder. I slid my arm over Maxie's back, hugging her closer.

Bucky fell to the ground. His face pointed toward us, bruised cheeks and split lip. The side of his head was bleeding. His eyes were open, searching. His gaze landed on me, pleading for it to stop. I longed for Stick or even

Father. They could do something, anything, to make it stop. Stick might run over, lending his fists to Bucky's defense. Father would know the right words, what to say that would help.

But not me.

I met Bucky's gaze and he knew. He saw me standing there, saw that I wasn't coming to his rescue, that he had been betrayed. I held his gaze, which was all I could manage to do. I read each moment, each thought that passed through him—when his mind was clouded with pain, when he found the strength to emit a silent plea for mercy. I knew the moment he gave up hoping. He could have looked away, could have shown anger at me for doing nothing. He didn't. He just looked at me and, God bless Bucky, he smiled.

Seeing that gentle smile, beneath all the blood and the sound of the beating, hit me hardest. Bucky closed his eyes. He didn't move at all, but they poked him with their nightsticks and kicked him a few more times.

Sirens wailed in the background, closing in with every whistle. Two squad cars fishtailed around the corner. The red lights flashed against the storefront windows.

The cops finally stopped kicking Bucky, cuffed him, and hauled him into the back of one of the police cars. Then they drove off.

People on the street began going about their business

again. The radio blasted, covering the silence of disbelief, of resignation. Maxie and I stood still as the car pulled away. The second cop car cruised slowly down the street, lights flashing. We averted our eyes, pretending not to notice.

"He never did anything to anyone," Maxie whispered as the car passed us.

"I know." I wrapped her mittened fingers in mine and she looked up at me. This wasn't how I'd wanted to hold her hand for the first time.

"What are we going to do?"

I shook my head. "I don't know."

I hurried home after Maxie went into her building. I made sure to check before I rounded any corners, and turned real wide along the sidewalks. I slipped inside my house and breathed deeply, drawing the warm, peppery aroma of Mama's chicken casserole into my lungs.

"How was your day?" Mama asked as I hung up my coat by the door and kicked off my shoes. She was sitting in the brown armchair beside the front windows, stitching buttons onto one of Father's shirts.

"All right." I flopped down on the couch. I hadn't meant to lie, but I couldn't say the truth out loud. I propped my stocking feet up on Mama's cherry coffee table.

Mama adjusted the shirt over her knees. She raised

one eyebrow and cleared her throat. I moved my feet to the carpet.

"In ten minutes, I need you to set the table."

I nodded and closed my eyes. Bucky's bruised-up face floated in front of me. I sat up. "I'll do it now."

Mama had already spread her green tablecloth over the dining table. She even had two candles, not lit, for the centerpiece. I picked silverware from the utensil drawer and dumped it on the tablecloth. My hands shook as I got down four plates from the cabinet by the sink. I laid them out around the table. The glasses waited in the drying rack on the counter. I grabbed all four of them at once, but one popped out of my grip. It cracked against the counter edge, tumbled to the floor, and shattered.

I knelt to pick up the pieces. Mama appeared in the kitchen doorway.

"Sam, don't touch that. Get out of there, with no shoes on. Look where you're stepping."

I stayed on my knees, staring at the broken glass. "I couldn't stop it, Mama, I didn't know what to do."

"Baby, don't fret yourself over one glass. We've got others. Get your shoes and just sweep it up."

My chest and stomach ached, but still I couldn't tell her. I swept up the glass while Mama pulled our dinner casserole out of the oven and put some rolls in to warm.

"Hello," Father called from the front door. He thumped around in the entryway, hanging his coat. I took my shoes back over there.

"Hi."

"Hi, Sam." Father smiled. "Where's your brother?" Stick's hook on the coatrack was empty. I shrugged. It was past our usual suppertime. Had he heard about Bucky already? News like this traveled fast in the neighborhood. If he'd found out, good. Then I wouldn't have to be the one to tell him. Maybe I wouldn't have to say anything about it, ever.

Mama left the dinner to warm while Father and I washed up, and we all waited for Stick. After a half hour Stick hadn't come home yet. Mama was worried sick over him. She didn't say anything, but she kept twisting her hands and looking out the front window. Finally, Father declared, "Let's eat."

We had finished dinner and were clearing the table when the doorbell rang. Mama raced from the kitchen and flung open the door. Fred and Leon came inside.

"Can I get either of you anything?" Mama said. "Chicken casserole? Something to drink?"

"No, thank you, Marjorie," Leon said. He faced Father. "We stopped by to talk for a moment. Sorry to interrupt supper."

"No intrusion. We're finished," Father said. "Sam was just about to start his homework." He gave me a pointed look. I rolled up the tablecloth and got my schoolbag. I spread my math homework out on the table and pretended to work on it as Mama cleared away the last of the supper dishes.

"It's Sharon Willis's boy, Clarence," Leon said. They took him into custody this afternoon."

Father motioned them into the living room. "Bucky? I know him. He used to be over here every day." He frowned. "He's a good kid. They arrested him?"

Leon grimaced and lowered his voice, glancing over at me. "They beat the living daylights out of him, Roland. For a while there, we weren't sure he'd even make it, but he's holding his own."

Father sat in silence for a moment, maybe saying a prayer. He finally spoke. "He's a tough kid. He'll make it. What's the charge?"

"Two counts of assaulting a police officer and resisting arrest."

My pencil skidded along the page.

Father raised his head. "Assault? Bucky?" His skeptical tone matched my thoughts. "I can't imagine him—"

"It sounds like he just snapped," Leon continued, shaking his head. "Maybe it has to do with his father. You never really get over a thing like that. At any rate, the kid attacked two police officers over on Bryant Street earlier this afternoon."

"That's not what happened," I blurted. "Bucky didn't start that fight, the police did!"

"Sometimes people act irrationally, Sam," Father said, turning toward me.

I stood up. "But Father, the police are lying."

"You don't know that, son. I realize Bucky is a friend of yours, but—"

"I do know! I was there. I saw it happen."

Father twisted in his seat to face me more fully. Mama set the casserole down with a *thunk*. Everyone stared at me. Then all of them started in at once.

"What are you talking about?"

"Are you saying—?"

"What have I told you about hanging out in the street?"

I traced the edge of the wood tabletop with my pencil eraser. "I was walking my friend Maxie home. She lives on Bryant Street and—"

Father frowned at my mention of that neighborhood. "Sam, I've told you a hundred times—"

"It wasn't after dark," I protested. "It was still the middle of the afternoon. Anyway, Maxie and I saw Bucky;

keklamagoon

he was on his way back to work from making a delivery. He was hurrying, and he looked over his shoulder when someone called his name, but he didn't stop running. He didn't even see them, he bumped into them by accident. They started yelling at him and hitting him with their sticks—"

"They drew nightsticks?" Father's eyebrows dropped lower and lower.

"For heaven's sakes, Roland, let the boy tell his story," Fred bellowed.

I nodded. "They had sticks. They talked to him, asked him his name and what he was running from. When he didn't answer all the questions, they started hitting him."

Fred and Leon glanced at each other. Father stared at me.

"There were plenty of people around who can tell you the same."

Father ran his hand over the top of his head. He turned to Leon. "Are you telling me no one came forward with this? Not one witness?"

"First I've heard of it," Leon said.

Father sighed. "Why didn't anyone say anything?"

"You know perfectly well why not, Roland," Leon said quietly.

Father nodded, rubbing the back of his neck. Fred

cleared his throat as if to say something, but sat back when Leon shook his head.

"There's something else we should discuss," Leon continued in a low voice. I strained to hear him. Leon glanced at me, then Mama. "Though now may not be the best time."

"Sam, go finish your homework," Father said. I stood up and gathered my school things as slowly as possible.

"Those kids, the Black Panthers, they're down at the police station now staging a protest," Leon said. "We didn't know what the purpose was, but hearing Sam"—all three men looked over at me—"it seems they might have cause."

I ducked around the corner into the hallway, but pressed up against the wall to listen.

"Roland—God, I don't know what to say here," Leon said.

"What is it, Leon?"

Fred's voice rang out loud and clear. "Steven is down there with them."

A wave of tension swept over the stillness.

The front door slammed. Fred's car started up in the driveway. I walked back into the living room, where Mama stood alone, looking after the men. We waited in silence.

CHAPTER 5

MAMA SENT ME TO BED AT THE USUAL time, but Father and Stick had not returned. I lay quietly, waiting. Then my gaze fell on the stack of magazines beneath Stick's bed. Forbidden territory, but this was an emergency.

I dug into the pile. *Time, Newsweek, National Geographic*. I rolled my eyes as I went through. No one else I knew read things like this, stuff that belonged on grown-ups' coffee tables. I almost stopped when I hit a volume of our encyclopedia, but right beneath it, there it was: *The Black Panther*. It was a different issue from before, the cover had a different look, but it was what I'd been looking for.

I settled back onto my bed, spreading the paper's narrow pages in front of me. "'The BPP,'" I read. I skimmed their ten-point platform, the list of things they planned to demand from the government:

1. We want freedom. We want power to determine the destiny of our Black Community.

2. We want full employment for our people.

3. We want an end to the robbery by the white man of our Black Community.

4. We want decent housing, fit for shelter of human beings.

5. We want education for our people that exposes the true nature of this decadent American society. We want education that teaches our true history and our role in this present day society.

6. We want all black men to be exempt from military service.

7. We want an immediate end to police brutality and the murder of black people.

8. We want freedom for all black men held in federal, state, county, and city prisons and jails.

9. We want all black people when brought to trial to be tried in court by a jury of their peer group or people from their black communities, as defined by the Constitution of the United States.

10. We want land, bread, housing, education, clothing, justice, and peace.

o o o

I read about Huey Newton, their founder and leader, who was in prison on murder charges, and about the "Free Huey" movement that had taken hold of Oakland and gotten everybody up in arms. Literally. The pictures showed black people in the ghettos with guns. Of course, there were always guns in the ghetto, but not like this. Not facing off with the police.

I tucked myself under the covers, as if going inside could protect me from the ideas in front of me. The articles were harsh but powerful, talking of a revolution with guns. Asking for a real war, saying it was the only way. It was so completely the opposite of everything I'd ever been taught, everything I'd ever done. It scared me, but I couldn't stop reading, couldn't stop imagining—what if it were possible, all these things that they wanted. Weren't these the things we all wanted?

I jumped when the front door slammed again. The picture frames shook on the wall. I sat up in bed.

"We're protesting again tomorrow," Stick's voice carried through the hallway. "And I'm going to be there."

"It's not appropriate for you to be involved with these militants. It is reckless behavior that I will not condone."

I grasped the sheets in my fists and held my breath.

"It doesn't have to be your way. It doesn't always have to be."

"Under this roof, you will do what you are told."

"I'll do whatever I want!"

"I am not going to discuss this further. Go to your room. Now."

Stick thumped into the room. He clicked the light on, and I pinched my eyes shut at the sudden brightness. When I opened them, Stick was tossing clothes around the room as he dressed for bed. His jacket landed on my bed, still cold from being outside. I pushed it off.

"What happened?"

"None of your business. Leave me alone." He shoved the dresser drawer shut so hard, the handles jangled against the wood.

"How's Bucky?"

Stick glared at me. "How about you leave me alone?"

"Come on," I said. "How is he? I saw what happened. I was really worried that he might—die or something."

"He didn't die. He's not going to die." He took a deep breath and studied me more closely. "What do you mean, you saw what happened?"

"I was there when they—I was walking Maxie home. We were talking to him just before the cops showed up."

"You talked to Bucky?"

"Yeah. He wanted me to—well, it doesn't matter." I leaned back against my pillow.

"What?"

"He wanted me to tell you that you should come by the shop tomorrow to talk. Said it was important. I don't know what it was about."

Stick's bedsprings creaked as he sat down. "It's okay. I know what he wanted. Why are you reading that?"

I didn't reply. It had to be pretty obvious why. But when he held out his hand for it, I passed it to him.

"Why are you?" I said quietly as I let it go. I knew he wouldn't answer me, either. Still, I felt glad he was here now; I didn't want to be alone. "What did Bucky want?"

Stick stared at his knees for a minute, then got up and turned the light off. "It doesn't matter now," he said as he got into bed. "Go to sleep."

I lay quietly for a few minutes, until I couldn't stand it any longer. "Stick?"

"Yeah?"

"You okay?"

Stick didn't say anything. I fell asleep waiting for him to answer.

In the morning, Stick was gone. At least now I knew where he probably was. The Breakfast. It still burned me that he hadn't told me about it to begin with, that I'd had to find out from Maxie. Didn't he trust me anymore?

"Mama!" I called. "Is my blue shirt clean? The one with the button pockets?"

Mama appeared in my doorway. "I just did the wash," she said. "Everything's back in the drawers. Put something on and come eat."

"I wanted to wear it to school," I groaned. I'd looked through my dresser twice, so I went to Stick's dresser, next to mine. Me and Stick already shared our socks because Mama couldn't tell them apart anymore, now that my feet had grown. I'd noticed some of his clothes mixed in with mine, so maybe she'd accidentally put mine in with his too.

I opened his drawers and dug for my shirt. Nothing. I settled on the floor and leaned against the dresser, trying to decide what else to wear. I'd already checked the closet, but maybe I should check again.

The block tower's hulking presence across the room distracted me. It was looking a bit ragged these days. Blocks poking out of alignment here and there. I'd have to do some quick repairs soon. Especially down at the bottom left. A small section of wall looked skewed, almost like it had come down and been rebuilt. I crawled over to take a closer look.

The crooked corner was in a short side section. It should have stood at a clean right angle to the main tower, but it was angled strangely, as if it had been hastily built. But there was nothing hasty about a five-year-old block tower. I freed a few bricks, preparing to realign the wall. Inside the gap, I spied a patch of green. Something was back there.

I loosened more bricks until I could make out the neatly folded piece of fabric hiding inside the block tower. One of Stick's shirts. Why was it in there? It made no sense at all.

I drew it out, carefully. It was slow to move, almost heavy. When it was free of the blocks, I picked it up, but it didn't come smoothly. It unfolded awkwardly and something rolled out of it, landing with a thump against the floor. A handgun!

I dropped the shirt as if it were too hot to touch. I shut the bedroom door softly, my hands leaning against the wood until the latch clicked. My knuckles found the lock and depressed it. My fingers lingered on the knob, waiting—for what?

I knelt in front of the tower again. My hands trembled as I reached, gently this time. Deliberately. I lifted the shirt away with two fingers.

I hadn't dreamed it. It was real. The dark metal seemed to gaze back at me, threatening even in its stillness. I could practically hear the twisted shout that was locked inside, waiting to be triggered, released.

I smoothed my finger across the nose and down the L of the handle. Cool, but not cold. Textured, but not rough.

I pulled my hand back and wiped it on my pant leg. What had I thought it would feel like?

With the edge of my fingernail, I eased the gun back inside the tower, uncovered. I restacked the blocks to shield it inside. Each piece I returned to its place made me feel worse. The tower seemed ugly now. Violated. All because of Stick, the one person I thought cared about what we had built as much as I did.

I slipped my arms into the sleeves of Stick's green shirt. It fit me better than I expected, but I paused in the middle of buttoning it. My stomach churned. The shirt I was putting on had just been wrapped around the gun. I almost took it off, but I didn't. I wore it as I collected my schoolbooks and packed my bag. I wore it while Mama kissed my cheek and wished me a nice day, and while Father watched me over the top of the morning paper as I put on my shoes and coat and slipped out the door. I wore it as I went out looking for Stick.

I found him after The Breakfast. He was standing against one of the side walls of the school building smoking a cigarette. Leaning nonchalantly against the bricks, he watched me come over. I weaved through groups of kids running and playing in the yard. I passed Maxie turning a jump rope for Bucky's sister Shenelle and some other little girls. Shenelle grinned and waved at me, waiting her turn to jump. I waved back and caught Maxie's eye. She gave me a half-smile and lifted one shoulder. Did Shenelle really understand what had happened to Bucky? Maybe it was better that she didn't.

"What do you tell Mama when you race out of the house every morning?" Stick said when I got close enough.

I glanced around. "What are you talking about?"

"She doesn't know you come here, does she? Do either of them?"

"I guess not. Why?"

Stick laughed. "'Cause you act like a bandit every time I see you here, like you're breaking somebody's rule. Why do you hide? You don't have to do everything Father wants, you know."

My stomach fluttered. "I don't know what he wants."

"For us to be what he is."

I kicked at some loose stones along the asphalt. "I don't know what that means."

"Yes, you do." He turned to me. "Is that what you want?"

We looked at each other for a while. "Maybe," I said.

Stick smiled. "Well, you can't be the rock and the river, Sam." Placing one hand against the bricks, he leaned toward me. "You're here, you're there, which is it?"

"It's just breakfast," I said. "Isn't it?" The last words

came out with more force than I'd intended. Stick's eyebrows went up. He nodded, chewing on the end of the cigarette.

"Since when do you smoke?"

Stick pulled the cigarette from his mouth and turned it over between his fingertips. He ground it out against the wall behind him. "I don't know."

"Father's not going to like it."

"He's not going to like a lot of things." That was for sure.

A basketball rolled up and bounced against my legs. Stick picked it up and tossed it back to a small boy with two missing front teeth. The boy ran back to his game, hugging the ball to his chest with spindly arms. Stick and I stood quiet, the children's energetic whoops and giggles swirling around us.

"What are you getting into, Stick?" The words came out of my mouth so quiet, Stick leaned a little toward me, like he was trying to hear better. Then he straightened up and turned away from me.

"Forget it."

"Don't give me your back." I grabbed his shirt, tried to make him turn around. He didn't.

"I found the gun."

Stick lowered his head for a moment. Then he turned toward me. His gaze flicked over the shirt I was wearing.

"Well? Say something," I said.

"You go through my stuff—twice, by the way—and now you've got the nerve to ask me about it?"

I pushed his shoulder. "The block tower is not *your* stuff."

A flash of something—guilt? regret?—crossed his face. He sighed. "I'm holding it for a friend, okay?"

"You know if Father finds out—"

Stick shot me a look fit for dirt and took off toward the tables. Of course I wouldn't tell on him, but it still bothered me.

"Hey," I called after him. He didn't turn around. I darted around the kids and caught up with him. "What am I supposed to do?"

"I've got work to do," Stick said.

Father was still all bent out of shape over yesterday's events. Throughout dinner he pumped me for details about Bucky's attack. "And you're certain they approached him first?"

I stared at the tablecloth. "He ran into them, but he didn't even mean to."

"Roland, that's enough now. Let the child eat." Mama trying to get Father to back off was like a daffodil standing in the path of a freight train. Sometimes she could hush him with a look or a tap on the arm, but tonight there was no stopping him.

"Just a few more questions," Father said.

I pushed the roast beef around on my plate so Mama wouldn't feel bad, but thinking about Bucky so hard made me lose my appetite.

"Leave him alone," Stick said. "Don't make him relive it." I glanced up at him, but he was looking at his plate. Suddenly, he was on my side?

"Steven, be quiet," Father said. Then he sighed. "Go to your room now, both of you." I hadn't really done anything wrong, but as long as I had to be in trouble, it felt good to be in it with Stick.

When we got to our room, Stick didn't glower at his desk and ignore me like he usually did when he was fighting with Father.

"Look, I need you to cover me for a little while," Stick said.

"Why should I?" I practically spat the words.

Stick raised his eyebrows at me. "I'm going out to the protest."

"No."

Stick shifted his weight from one foot to the other and crossed his arms. "Sam."

"Are you taking it with you?" We locked eyes. I didn't

back down against Stick's stormy gaze like I usually did. Right then, I didn't care. I didn't want him to leave me alone with it.

His eyes narrowed as he realized I wasn't going to let him pretend he didn't know what I was talking about. He sat down on his bed and pulled on his shoes. "No. I can't."

"Well, you can't leave it here."

"Sam, stop it. It's none of your business."

"It's my room too. What are you going to do if Mama finds it?"

Stick stood up. "Don't even joke about that."

"Who's joking? I found it, didn't I?"

"Keep your voice down." Stick sighed. "Look, I don't have anywhere else to put it right now. Just forget about it."

Right. Sure. I flopped down onto my bed, facing away from him. What was I supposed to do? I couldn't tell on him. I didn't even want to, but how was I supposed to act normal with that thing in my room? Why couldn't I be casual about it, the way Stick was?

"So, you'll cover for me, then?" He was already pulling on his jacket. He pushed the curtains aside.

I rolled over. "How am I supposed to do that? You know I can't lie."

"Say good night without opening the door, that kind of thing. I'll be back in a bit."

"Is Bucky in the Panthers too? Is that why they're protesting?"

Stick frowned and stood up straighter. "No, it's not why. Nobody cares if Bucky's a Panther or not. We care that what happened to him was wrong."

"So he's not a Panther?"

Stick smiled a little. "You know Bucky. He wouldn't carry a gun if you paid him, much less use it."

I smiled back. "Yeah." I wanted to add, You either, I thought.

Stick raised the window. "Don't lock it. I'll knock if I can't get it up from outside."

I opened my mouth to say I won't, but I didn't. Stick paused, one leg already outside. It would show him, all right, if I locked the window behind him. But we both knew I wouldn't.

"See you," I said instead as he slipped out the window. I caught a glimpse of his face as he disappeared. Something in his expression said he was leaving more than me behind.

Not five minutes later, Father knocked at the door. "Good night, Sam. Good night, Steve," he called.

"Good night," I called back.

Father's breath in the hallway. "Sam?"

"Yes?"

"Open the door, please."

It was all over now. "Um, we're in bed. We're going to sleep."

Father turned the doorknob. It had been pointless to lock it. He would just have made me open it, anyway. "Where's your brother?"

Wherever he was, he was about to owe me big. "I'm not sure."

Father pointed at Stick's bed. "The minute he comes back, I want to know, understood?"

If he thought I was going to rat on Stick . . . there was no way.

"Sam?"

I couldn't speak.

Father sighed. "Never mind." He left the room.

Several minutes later, through the wall, came muffled sounds of him talking with Mama. The walls weren't thin enough to hear normal conversations, only raised voices, so they had to be arguing.

"Go back and talk to him," Mama said.

Father said something in response. A moment later he came in, carrying one of the big pillows off his and Mama's bed. He had removed his belt and shoes and unbuttoned his shirt, revealing his white undershirt. He placed the pillow against the side of Stick's bed, then flicked off the light and sat down on the floor.

I crossed my legs on the bed and leaned against the wall. A thin stream of light from the window lit a long rectangle over Father's face and chest. I liked him being there with me, even though it meant I had failed Stick.

"Are you going to sit there until he comes back?"

"Your brother is very angry with me right now," Father said, tugging at his shirt buttons.

"He's mad about other things too," I said.

Father raised his eyes to me. "Yes, I know."

"Bucky's one of his best friends."

"I hate what happened to Bucky, Sam. It makes me angry too, but, son, anger makes people foolish. You have to find a way to control it, because people will take advantage of any opening you give them."

Could I tell him I was mad too? Mostly at myself. I'd been right there, but I had done nothing to help Bucky. I hadn't even tried. Stick would've known what to do. He wouldn't have just stood there. I tipped my head back and closed my eyes. "Everything's a mess."

"Things are changing, Sam. It takes time."

"How much longer?"

Father smiled. "If you could bottle and sell that answer, you'd be a millionaire in no time." He crossed his arms and stared out the window. "Every day I wake up thinking if I knew what tomorrow would look like, it would make today a whole lot easier. Change is never easy. When this whole thing started, we didn't think it would take as long as it has."

"How can you be sure it will happen?"

Father shook his head. "Faith and perseverance got us this far. They'll take us the rest of the way."

We sat in silence for a few moments, then Father rested his head back against Stick's mattress. "Go to sleep, Sam."

I slid under the covers and lay down facing him.

"Good night." Through my eyelashes I watched him watching me fall asleep. I tried to imagine the world as it should be, the way Father could surely see it in his mind.

CHAPTER 6

I DIDN'T HEAR STICK COME IN THAT NIGHT, OR hear what Father had to say about him sneaking out. I woke in the morning to rustling sounds in the room. It was barely light outside, too dim even to read the clock on my desk without crawling to the end of the bed to look. I lay still. Stick riffled through papers at his desk, then tiptoed to the dresser and eased open a drawer. He changed his clothes, putting on an outfit I'd never seen and couldn't totally make out in the dark. It looked like some kind of one-piece suit or overalls.

"You going to The Breakfast?" I asked.

Stick jumped. "You're up."

"Yeah, I thought there was an elephant in the room."

Stick didn't smile. "Sorry. Go to sleep."

"I have to go to school."

"Not for a few hours, Sam. Sleep." He opened the

window. He came and went more that way than through the door lately.

"Okay. See you at The Breakfast."

Stick hesitated, one leg out the window. "Not today."

I sat up. "What? Where are you going?"

"Sleep." He touched my shoulder, then slid outside.

For weeks, the same thing. Stick left early, trying not to wake me. I always woke up. I pretended to sleep, lying very still but keeping my eyes open. Where was Stick going every day? He never came to The Breakfast anymore and he refused to talk to me or answer my questions, even though I hadn't done anything to him. Bucky was still in jail. His trial would start soon. Father was organizing a demonstration. All the while, Stick grew quieter and somehow more still. A shadow crossed his face whenever anyone mentioned Bucky, and every day it seemed to stay longer, pressing his features into a perpetual frown.

Maxie and I walked and talked every day after school, and I started liking her more and more. Spring weather set in, and on one of the first warm afternoons, Maxie and I stayed late at school watching some kids playing ball in the schoolyard.

"Finally, it's spring!" Maxie cheered, spinning across the pavement. She danced, and I leaned against the fence. She'd retired the mittens until next winter, and her slender, graceful hands waved above her head. I laughed out loud at her crazy twirling. She was pretty much the only thing that made me smile these days. We stayed in the yard until Mr. Baker, the principal, emerged from the school.

"All you kids, get home, now!" he called out across the yard as he locked the building. He shooed us out of the playground while we complained that it wasn't even late yet.

I walked Maxie home, and when I left her, it was nearly dark. People seemed to be milling around more than usual, probably because of the good weather. I looked around. The crowds were growing. People streamed out of the buildings into the streets. "What's happening?" I asked someone rushing past.

"King is dead," the man shouted, then ran on.

"What?" I yelled after him. I spun around. "What's going on?"

"He's dead," a woman's voice came from my left. She was slight, dark-skinned, and holding the hand of a little boy.

"Who's dead?"

"Dr. King. They shot him. Someone shot Dr. King." Her voice was clear; I caught every word this time, but it couldn't be true.

"No," I said.

The woman clapped a hand over her mouth. Tears came to her eyes. "Oh, Lord," she said through her fingers. "Lord in heaven." She scooped up the boy and hurried off through the crowd. As she left, individual shouts and people's crying separated from the general roar of the crowd.

From a passing car radio, the news blared out and echoed between the sidewalks. "Breaking news. Prominent civil rights leader Dr. Martin Luther King, Jr., died tonight in Memphis after being shot while standing on the balcony of his hotel. Dr. King was taken . . ." The voice faded and blurred into nothing.

I stood senseless for a moment, sure I'd heard something wrong. Dr. King couldn't die. No one would let that happen. Just last night we'd listened to part of his latest speech on the radio. He'd talked about the future, said he'd seen the promised land and we were on our way. He'd been fine then, just last night. I couldn't believe it, and yet somehow, I knew it was true.

My mind cluttered with memories. Out of the gray dusk, they appeared. Dr. King's face, his voice, his presence. Dr. King, fist pounding the pulpit when he preached at our church once last year. Dr. King pacing in the hotel corridor, thinking about a big upcoming speech. Dr. King standing on the Lincoln Memorial steps on that same hot August day. Dr. King walking not six blocks from here, leading a rally for affordable housing. Dr. King at the dinner table, eating chicken pot pie from our good china plates.

I bent in the middle, holding my stomach. I thought I might be sick. I searched the faces around me. There was an edginess to the crowd, as if we were all waiting for something to happen. It hung in the air—the promise of something horrible, as if the news wasn't horrible enough.

When the restless energy in the street ignited, everything busted out into the open. Sadness and anger curled through the street, a wave of hurt. It tasted bitter, it looked ugly.

Glass was breaking, raining down like tears against the asphalt. Things fell all around me, inside me, until it seemed there was nothing left. A shattered store window lay glistening at my feet. I stared at the wreckage. Feet and bodies rushed past, bumped against me. A scratching sound beside me. A boy striking a match. The tiny flame glowed as he lit the mouth of a Molotov cocktail. The flame seared the tip of the oiled cloth and sizzled toward the bottleneck. He hurled it, and the fire spread across the storefront in front of us. The boy spat into the pile of glass at our feet. He turned to me, a glistening light in his eyes. His gaze burned as hot as the fires around us, fueled by anger, helplessness, desperation. I saw my reflection in his eyes. If I stood still any longer I might catch fire too.

The shouts and pandemonium filled my head. Fire,

crowds, broken things everywhere. Logic urged me to run, get away, but something kept me there. Another fire burned somewhere close by. The heat rose up and held me. It pressed close to me, pushed its way inside. I surrendered to the wave, to the fire. I picked up a brick from the sidewalk and flung it through the store window, then I rushed at the building. The heat dug deep in my chest; it overpowered everything else, the confusion, the pain, the questions. I let the fire take over. I kicked the door until it caved in. I didn't know why. Because I was there, because it felt less bad. Less bad than doing nothing.

"Sam!"

I turned. Maxie stood a few feet away. I dropped the pipe I held. It clattered to the street and rolled away. I rushed toward her, but tripped and fell. Broken glass stabbed my fingers, tore the knees of my pants. I stood up and reached for Maxie.

We raced through the streets, hand in hand. Everything was on fire. The heat was all around me, in me. I wanted to curl up in the street and burn. I stumbled, but Maxie held me tight. Her face was streaked with tears and sweat.

She pulled me into the alley behind George's Liquor Cabinet. We leaned against the rough bricks and breathed hard, staring at each other. Would tomorrow come? If it did, what would it look like? Maxie and I stood still and held each other. There was nothing else to do. She cried into my shoulder. I had to protect her, keep her safe from all the mess around us.

"Come on," I said. "We're going home." I tucked her under my arm and guided her to the street. She wrapped her arms around my chest. A surge of feeling rushed through the empty space inside me. I kissed her moist cheek. She hugged me tighter.

Police sirens and flashing lights surrounded us. The air smelled of sweat and ashes. It was hard to walk fast and stand so close, so I took her hand instead. We hurried on, fingers locked together, toward my house. We tripped in the door, breathing hard. Mama looked up from the television. She sat on the edge of the chair by the window, fingers curled deep into the armrests. Father shouted into the telephone from the kitchen.

"Oh, baby," Mama said. "Baby." She stretched out trembling hands to me. I went over and she pulled me down, pressing my face into her neck. I tugged away, but Mama took hold of my arms. My palms were scratched from the glass, so she held the backs of my hands and surveyed the damage. Then she looked past me to Maxie, reached for Maxie's hand and squeezed it.

"There was nowhere else to go," Maxie said, looking between Mama and me.

Mama nodded. "Stay with us." She turned back to gaze at the television. The reporter's flat voice sent chills through me.

"Let's turn it off," I said to Maxie. She shook her head.

"We have to hear," Mama said. "We have to hear."

"What's left to hear, Mama? He's dead," I whispered. Her grip on me went slack, and I freed myself from her fingers.

"Hush, child." Mama stared at me without blinking. She knew, but she didn't want to hear me say it. Maxie and I moved to the sofa, and I held her hand again. She leaned against me. We sat without speaking, watching the newscaster report the facts over and over, as if at some point the story would change.

From time to time I glanced at Maxie. Each time, it seemed, she wasn't paying attention to the television news. She was looking around the room, at the furniture and the wallpaper, at Father's large, cluttered desk, at the framed pictures on the walls. The hand that wasn't caught in mine stroked the soft fabric of the sofa cushions intently.

Eventually, Mama moved to the edge of her chair, her fingers wrapped firmly around the armrests. "Well, that's enough of that," she declared with false brightness. She snapped off the television set and turned to Maxie. "What's your phone number, honey? I'll call your mother and let her know you're safe."

Maxie lifted her head from my shoulder, pulling away from me. "No, that's okay." She looked alarmed. "I'll just go home now."

"Nonsense," Mama said. "You're not going anywhere tonight. You'll stay with us."

Maxie bent over and fumbled with her shoes. I nudged her arm, but she wouldn't look at me.

"Give her the number," I said. "You can't go back out there."

Maxie looked at her knees. "We don't have a phone," she mumbled. My face flushed. I hadn't known. I hadn't even thought of it. Maxie finally raised her head, but this time I looked away, embarrassed.

"That's all right, Maxie." Father emerged from the kitchen doorway. "I have to go out, anyway. I'll stop by and tell your mother myself."

"Roland, no."

Father strode across the room and kissed Mama's cheek. "I have to take care of a few things." Despite the attempt at his typical, casual confidence, Father seemed flustered. He let Mama sneak her arms around him and lay her head on his chest instead of breaking away to get on with the business at hand. He held her longer than he might on a normal day.

Maxie related her address, and Father nodded, but he wasn't looking at her. He was looking at me. I couldn't tell what he was thinking. I wouldn't have wanted to guess.

He thumped out the door and the three of us sat in silence. I remembered what the journey here with Maxie had been like. Things tend to get worse, not better, and knowing how unbalanced I'd felt being in the midst of the fray, I couldn't imagine the state of the streets right now.

We sat there for a long time, sometimes talking quietly, but mostly resting in silence. Father returned and we were still sitting there. His face was haggard, I noticed with alarm. He traipsed in heavily, as if his boundless stamina for pursuing justice had been exhausted. The thought of that shook me.

"What are you all still doing up?" he murmured.

None of us had a good answer for that. Mama stretched. "I don't know, and it's past time we went to sleep. I'll just make up the sofa now for Maxie."

"No," Father said. "Take her to the bedroom. I have some more calls to make. I'll sleep on the sofa."

Mama stood up and approached him. "You need to rest."

This time he evaded her embrace. "I will," he said. Her eyes followed his back as he went to his desk and shuffled papers around.

I walked Maxie and Mama to Mama's room. They crawled into the bed beside each other, still wearing all their clothes. Mama turned on her side, facing the wall. Maxie lay down tentatively, looking like she felt out of place. I kissed Mama on the cheek, then rounded the bed and kissed Maxie on the mouth. It just happened. I opened my eyes wide and tried to look like it had been an accident, or a mistake, in case she wanted it to be. But she didn't seem to mind it. She even smiled, as much as anyone could smile that night.

As I headed to bed, I peeked into the living room. Father stood at the window, pulling back the curtains every few moments to look out. I lay in bed staring at the ceiling, trying not to think about anything, but my stomach churned and my eyes kept tearing up. The sounds of Mama weeping came through the wall. Was Maxie crying too? Could she ever fall asleep in a strange house? The floorboards creaked as Father paced.

Stick never came home.

"Sam." I woke to Stick's hand on my shoulder. "Sam!"

"What?" I rubbed my eyes. Why was he waking me up? I cracked one eyelid. A hint of predawn cast the room in shades of light blue. Stick knelt beside my bed, a strange look on his face.

I sprang up and grabbed Stick's shoulder. "Was it a dream?"

Stick shook his head, eyes heavy. His face seemed to have new angles, a tightness I didn't recognize. My fingers dug into the buttery, cool fabric of his jacket. Leather. With a crisp collar and two rows of buttons down the front.

"Where were you?"

"Shh! Don't wake the whole house."

"I didn't think I would ever fall asleep," I said. "I was waiting for you. Where have you been?"

"There's still rioting. The projects are a mess." Stick shifted his weight to his other knee.

I rubbed my forehead. "Everything's burning."

Stick grabbed my hand away from my face. "What happened to you?"

"Fell in broken glass," I murmured.

"Where?" He looked in my face. "Don't tell me—What were you thinking going down there?" He stood up and smacked me lightly on the side of my head. "Sam."

I tugged at a loose thread on my bedspread. "I had to get Maxie home. Things just started happening. I don't know."

"She got home all right?"

"She's here. We couldn't get to her building. I didn't know what to do. I can't believe this is happening." I swallowed hard.

Stick laid his hand on my head. "It's all right, Sam."

My throat felt tight. I kicked off my covers and moved out from under his hand. "No, it's not. Stick, why didn't you come home?"

"I was with some friends."

I could guess which ones. "What did you tell Father?"

"He doesn't know I'm here. I have to get back. I just wanted to make sure things were fine over here." Stick moved to the window. He slid the panes up and stuck his leg out, then he slipped into the dusky morning.

Once on the ground, he leaned back in. The faint sun rays at his back cast his face in shadows. "Don't tell them I was here."

"Stick, wait." But he was gone.

Reverend Downe held a memorial service for Dr. King at our church a few days later. Everybody came. By the time the service started, people were standing on the steps outside, pushing to get in. We sat in our usual row, Father, Mama, Stick, and me, smashed all up against one another. I folded the stack of tissues Mama handed me and slid them into the breast pocket of my suit. I wasn't going to need them.

"Good afternoon, friends," Reverend Downe began. "Thank you for joining me today. When tragedy strikes, we must not forget to take time to breathe, to pray, to mourn. Now, let us take the time to remember the Reverend Dr. Martin Luther King Jr. We have lost a leader, a brother, and with him, a piece of ourselves. Because Dr. King carried a piece of each of us in him. Today, we take the time to recognize that a piece of him remains alive in each of us as well. Today, we must not only mourn his death, we must celebrate his life."

Reverend Downe's sermon brought the house down. I'd never seen so many tears in one room. The sobbing mixed with the constant hum of "Lord Jesus" and "Amen." Dr. King was one of the only people who basically everyone had to respect, no matter what.

I still couldn't believe he was dead. For as long as I could remember, most everything about our lives had been pointed toward him, toward the movement. What would happen now? Dr. King's speeches and his life were all about peace and brotherhood, about finding justice. And we listened. Yet, all we had learned was that when you stand up, you get shot down.

Mama kept reaching over and squeezing my hand. Was she trying to comfort me or herself? Either way, it didn't help. Her fingers pressed against the cuts along the sides of my hand, reminding me of things that hurt.

The choir began singing "We Shall Overcome," and

everybody joined in. Everybody but me and Stick.

In the midst of the familiar refrain, a voice behind me broke from the chorus. I turned around. Somebody's short, wrinkled grandma stood there, eyes folded shut, hands raised with the Spirit, murmuring over and over, "We're ready for the overcoming, Lord. We been singing for it long enough."

I turned back front, but I could still see her, swaying with a rhythm of her own. I mouthed the words, because Father was watching, but no sound came out of my throat. "We shall overcome," my lips whispered. The tune hung empty over my ears; the words tasted stale in my mouth. Then they slipped away, and I couldn't find them again.

Mama cried softly on the way home. The weather had turned cold again, nearly overnight, as if even the sky knew something terrible had happened.

We drove past the school, past the edge of the park. Stick slid down in his seat so his knees touched the back of Father's seat. Beyond the park's chain-link fence, a small crowd gathered. I recognized some of them—Raheem, guys from the breakfast, guys from school. They wore leather jackets, like the one Stick had worn into our room the other night.

A tall man with a smooth Afro stood on a crate, speaking

through a bullhorn over the people. "The cops don't own this neighborhood."

"No, they don't!" the crowd called.

"The cops don't rule this block."

"Not this block!" On the other side of the park, a police squad car rolled slowly past, blipping the lights and siren every few moments. The crowd made no move to disperse.

My pulse sped up. I knew what could happen, and I didn't want to see it. I couldn't stand to witness another awful thing. Yet I couldn't tear my eyes away.

"Who rules this block?" the man on the crate said.

Fists raised. "We do!"

"Who owns this 'hood?"

"We do!"

"Let me hear it."

They punched the sky. "We do!"

The leader's head bobbed up and down in rhythm. "That's right, sisters and brothers. We are not slaves any longer."

"No, we ain't!"

"We must not let them hold us to a lower standard. We must hold ourselves to a higher standard."

Father steered the car around the corner, heading away from the park. "Those kids are going to get themselves killed," he muttered. The words dug into me, their truth and their wrongness colliding deep in my chest.

Stick breathed on the glass, watched it fog up, then dragged his knuckles through the slick grayness. His eyes flicked to the back of Father's head, then dropped. The scar line on his forehead twitched and tightened. They weren't in the same car. They weren't even on the same road.

CHAPTER 7

THE NEXT DAY, FATHER FLEW TO ATLANTA to attend the real funeral service, the one with the coffin and the crowd. Mama and I watched it on television. Mama's hands twisted against each other as we watched. She was going to get wrinkles from all that wringing.

Stick was out.

I couldn't stand being in the house either, so I went looking for Maxie. The streets were still a mess. A lot of stores were closed. Others had nailed sheets of plywood or metal in place of missing windows. The gutters, a mess of glass and garbage. If anything beautiful had ever existed here, it was long gone. Gone from people's eyes, and from the very air they breathed. Only the ugliness remained. The only tangible mood was as a swirling drain, sucking away any remnants of hope. The stink of ashes lingered in the humid air. People moved like shadows. The rain-cloud sky painted everything an uncertain gray.

An elderly couple swept up broken glass and debris along the sidewalk in front of their barbershop/beauty parlor. The woman dragged the thin broom with slow, deliberate strokes. The man bent low, holding a sheet of cardboard as a dustpan for her. I slowed, because I felt sure he would crumple to the ground. But he straightened, balancing the cardboard long enough to dump the load into a trash bin. He sighed with accomplishment while she readied a new pile, then he bent again into their slow waltz of sorrow. I should have stopped to help them, but I couldn't let myself do more than see.

I found Maxie sitting with a group of girls in front of her building. She leaped to her feet when she saw me, breaking away from her friends.

"I have to get away from here," she said, gazing up at me with eyes that were holding back tears. I hugged her, partly because I didn't want her to see the shame I suddenly felt. I was glad I'd come, but I'd been selfish, thinking only that Maxie would make me feel better. Things must have been even worse for her. I hated seeing the neighborhood in shambles, but it wasn't my home.

Maxie and I went down to the park near the school. She took my hand as we walked, her soft fingers gripping the edges of my palm. Neither of us had much to say. We sat on a thin metal bench and watched squirrels dart between the budding trees.

"Raheem is with the Panthers now," she said at last.

"I thought he always was."

"It's different now." She pushed her hair over her shoulders, her fingers twisting through the curled black strands. "It's just different."

"Yeah." Stick had been gone more than ever lately. The house was quiet, everything in it a reminder of things now lost.

Maxie rolled her lips in and out. "I'm really afraid now, Sam," she whispered. "Are you?"

"A little," I admitted. She leaned her head against my chest and I laid my arm over her shoulders. "I don't know what's going to happen."

"What does your dad say?"

I sighed. "He thinks nothing's changed. 'All the more reason to press forward.' 'We shall—'" I couldn't say it.

The top of Maxie's head brushed against my chin. "We shall overcome?"

"Yeah, that."

Maxie pulled away from me. "There's a meeting on Wednesday."

The thousand thoughts swarming inside me cried out in unison at her soft words. I took her hands. "I'll be there."

o o o

Right away, I regretted walking into the house. Father and Stick stood at opposite sides of the dining table, heaving deep breaths and glowering at each other. Stick wore his black jacket, his shades resting on top of his head. Mama was in the kitchen, not slicing the vegetables laid out on the counter. She looked through the doorway at me as I came into the living room.

"How can you not be angry?" Stick shouted.

"Of course I'm angry. You know how I feel—felt—about Martin. What's been done is utterly reprehensible. But we have to go on."

"Go on with what?" Stick cried out.

"You've got to hold on to that anger, son." Father leaned forward, hands balled in fists at his chest. "Let it burn, let it fan the flames of your will, your determination. The movement is bigger than one man, Steven. Martin would tell you that."

Stick took off his shades and slung them onto the table. They clattered along the wood and came to rest against Father's newspaper.

"It's over," Stick said. "Everyone knows it."

"You don't stop fighting because of a setback, even this one. If anything, it's a reason to keep going." Father's voice vibrated with intensity.

"I'm not saying stop; no one is saying stop," Stick cried, throwing out his arms. "I'm talking about putting up a real fight."

"We are fighting, son. It's a long road."

Stick grabbed the sides of his head, digging his fingers into his hair. "It's not happening. Dr. King tried the peaceful way. They came back at him with bullets. They brought this war on us! It's time to fight back."

Father shook his head. "No son of mine is getting mixed up in that."

Stick leaned forward, planting his fists on the tabletop. His eyes bored into Father's. "Then I ain't your son." The words dropped from his lips like boulders.

"Don't talk back to me," Father said, his voice rising. "I don't want to hear—"

"I'm a Panther." Stick broke through Father's tirade with a calm breath.

Father sucked in his belly, sucked back the words that would have come next. "Not in my house," he said instead.

Stick lifted his fists from the table and stepped back. Father lowered himself back into his chair. They stared at each other. The clock didn't tick. My heart didn't beat. Mama pressed her hips against the counter.

Stick lifted his shades from the dining table and slid them over his eyes. Father sat still, a carved, immovable statue. Stick crossed the living room without a sound and without a glance in my direction. I tried to call his name, but my voice caught in my throat.

Stick slammed the door, and I knew what forever sounded like.

I let go of the couch and raced after him. I caught him at the end of the driveway and ran in front, stopping him with my hand against his chest.

"What are you doing?" I yanked the glasses off his face. Stick glared at me as he lifted them right back out of my hand. He held out his arms, the shades dangling from his fingers.

"I'm leaving. It's about time, anyway. Get back inside before he kicks you out too."

"He's not kicking you out. You can't leave. Where you gonna go?"

"I got places." Stick pushed forward, past me.

I grabbed his arm. "What about me? You can't do this."

"I don't have a choice anymore, Sam."

"You always have a choice." Father's words, coming out of my mouth.

"We both know that's a lie." He tugged out of my grip. "The truth is, you do what you have to do." Stick slipped on his shades, tapped the side of my arm with his fist, then walked away.

I didn't know how to follow him this time. I'd been standing too still for too long. Stick didn't look back. Once he turned the corner, I backed up the driveway, my eyes locked on the place I'd last seen him before he disappeared.

I walked back into a different house. I pushed through the stillness, like a blur in a slow-motion picture.

Mama stood in the kitchen doorway, arms at her sides, loosely clutching a vegetable knife in her fingers. She stared at me with dry eyes. Father and Mama watched me come in alone, but neither of them asked after Stick. The silence seemed unbreakable. As I closed the door, the soft *click* of the latch exploded in the air. Mama jumped as if it had been a gunshot. The knife slid to the ground with a sharp ping against the tile.

Without another word, Father laid his head down on the table and wept. The sound of it shook every part of me. I clutched the doorknob in my fist, leaned my back against the cool wood. The order of the universe had changed.

C H A P T E R 8

SAT AT THE DINING TABLE STARING AT MY MATH homework, but it wasn't coming together like usual. I couldn't concentrate. I was supposed to meet Maxie in an hour for the Wednesday night class. I was on the last problem, but I kept messing it up. I'd gotten X easy enough, but I couldn't figure out what Y was supposed to be. I scribbled out the numbers and started again.

"Why what, baby?"

I jumped about a mile. Mama stood frowning over me, a steaming mug in her hand.

"What?"

"You just said, 'I don't know why.'"

"I'm talking to myself. Algebra."

"Hmm." She held the cup under her nose and sniffed the steam.

"Is that cocoa?"

She shook her head, extending the cup toward me. "Chamomile."

I wrinkled my nose, and Mama laughed. "Your cocoa's on the counter," she said. She sat down across from me, gathering the edges of her housecoat in her lap.

I put down my pencil and rubbed the sides of my face. "You put in an extra sugar cube?"

Mama shot me a look. "I know how my boys like their cocoa." She dropped her eyes and wrapped both hands around her mug. Her thumbs tripped over each other, running up and down along the handle.

I went into the kitchen. My cocoa mug sat steaming on the counter, next to Stick's empty one. The pan of hot milk still rested on the stove burner, just enough there for a second mug. I poured it out in the sink and put Stick's mug back in the cupboard. I lifted my mug and stirred the spoon.

Mama was watching me through the door as I returned to the table. "How is your brother doing?" she said, her voice quieter than usual. Stick had been gone three days, but they hadn't yet talked to me about what happened.

"I don't know. He's probably fine."

"Where is he staying?"

I shrugged. Mama hunched forward and her frown deepened. "He hasn't been going to school."

I shrugged again. She would know better than me. "We don't see each other at school." Except for sometimes at the breakfast, and I wasn't about to tell Mama that. Tomorrow morning, she'd be waiting down there, ready to drag Stick home by the ear.

"He'll come back," I said.

Mama shook her head. "He's just like his father."

"He's nothing like Father," I said.

Mama lifted her mug. "No, baby, they're the same. Exactly the same. Stubborn. Focused." She sipped her tea. "Not a bone of compromise in either of them."

True enough. "Where is Father, anyway?" I hadn't seen him at all since I'd come home from school. Not that I was complaining. If he was here, he'd be breathing down my neck until I finished my homework.

"He's probably out looking for your brother."

I glanced up.

Mama's mouth twitched over the rim of her mug. "I told you, stubborn."

The wall clock read 6:15. Class started in fifteen minutes. "Mama, do you mind if I go out for a little while?"

"It's after dinner, Sam."

"My homework's done." I wrote $Y=42$ under my scribbled out equation. Who cared if it was the wrong answer?

"Just where do you plan to go at this hour?"

"I'm supposed to meet up with Maxie."

Mama's fingers hugged her teacup. She took a slow sip. "You know what your Father would say."

"I know." I held my breath.

"Why do you think I'll say something different?" She spoke in her sweetest voice, but it wasn't a question.

"Please, Mama."

"Sam, you know the rules of this house." The twinge of sadness in her voice suddenly seemed to be about more than Stick being gone, but I wasn't sure what else it meant.

There was no point in arguing it further. Mama had her own kind of stubbornness. I scooped up my homework and headed to my room. I grumbled to myself as I left the table. I was going to stand Maxie up and miss my first political education class, to boot. A big part of me was relieved. Mama had given me a perfect excuse not to go. But there was something nagging deep inside of me that grew stronger by the moment. I couldn't explain it or define it, but there were things I needed to understand. A part of me that would no longer sit still and do as I was told.

By the time I reached my room, I had a plan.

I dropped my books on my bed, took my spare jacket from the closet, and went to the window. I raised the sash and stuck my leg out, then paused to listen for Mama.

The evening air cooled my hot face as I climbed the rest

of the way outside. I stood in the grass, my hands on the windowsill, thrilling in the rush of freedom. Had Stick felt this way every day? No, he probably got used to it a long time ago. I listened into the house for one more minute, then I hurried out across the lawn.

I unbuttoned my coat right away as I walked into the meeting. People packed the tiny room, and the air felt as thick as the crowd. Stick stood near the front. I wormed my way through rows of metal folding chairs, my eyes on his back. As I came up beside him, people shifted, knocking me into Stick. He turned his head and his face took on a mix of expressions, real annoyed like when we were little and I tried to tag along with him and his friends, but also glad to see me, I could tell. I was glad to see him, too.

Stick slammed his shoulder back into mine. "What are you doing here?"

I pushed him again. "What does it look like?" Then I added, "Where have you been?"

"Around." We were shoving each other, for no real reason, but it felt right. A kid standing by Stick shot us a dirty look, so we stopped. I checked Stick over. Three days away from home, and he seemed none the worse for wear. He actually looked pretty smooth and official, dressed up in his black leather jacket, combat boots, and beret.

Stick shoved his hands in his pockets. "So, how are . . . things?" He stared at his feet and wouldn't look at me.

I hesitated. "Strange," I said. That was the truth.

"Yeah?"

"Quiet." Uncomfortable. Lonely.

"Mama, she's all right?"

I took a deep breath. Should I tell him she cries every night? His eyes said he didn't want to know the real story.

"Mama's fine." My smile felt stiff. "Misses you."

Stick tucked his hands under his arms. "Yeah, I guess. Father?"

"He's fine." I paused. He waited. "We don't talk about it."

Stick nodded. "I figured that." He reached up and adjusted his beret. I felt heavy, stuffed to bursting with all the things we weren't saying. All the thoughts I couldn't bring aloud, like how mixed up the world had become and why couldn't he be there to help me figure it out. Instead, we just stood there, pretty awkwardly for two guys who'd spent our whole lives sharing a bedroom. I hadn't even put a block on the tower since Stick left. I wanted to tell him that, but I couldn't. Our room might be the same as it had always been, but we weren't.

"Hey, can we get started?" A tall, thin guy at the front

of the room waved his hands, motioning people to sit down. He looked a few years older than Stick, maybe twenty-one or so. "Find a seat, any seat, and sit yourself in it," he said, a hint of musical rhythm to his speech. His lips tipped up in a smile that made it seem he was talking just to me.

"Who's that?" I whispered.

"Leroy Jackson," Stick said. "He's talking tonight. Go on and sit with your girl before she loses your seat."

Maxie motioned to me from across the room, her hand on the empty seat beside her. She was arguing with another girl over the chair. "See you," I said, heading toward her. She looked relieved to see me approaching.

"Hey, that's my seat," I said to the girl trying to pry Maxie's fingers from the metal. She shot me some kind of ghetto death stare, but backed off.

"About time," Maxie said as I fell into the seat. "What were you doing?"

"Sorry. I had to talk to him for a minute." I cupped her hand in both of mine, drawing comfort from the warm softness of her fingers between mine.

"Oh, please. Talk to your brother when you get home. Talk to me now." She flashed her charming smile. I drew her arm across my stomach, tucking her elbow inside mine. She came close willingly, and it felt nice. She was with me, even if no one else was.

Maxie tipped her head, a question in her eyes. I hadn't told her about Stick walking out. I kept thinking he'd come home. Seeing him here, I wasn't sure anymore. "Maxie, I have to tell you—"

"Okay, everybody, welcome to this week's political education class," Leroy Jackson said. "I see a lot of new faces out there tonight. It's great that you all came down. Looks like my boys are doing a good job spreading the word."

Stick and some other bereted guys stood against the wall to my right. Leroy perched himself on the edge of a desk at the front of the room. Behind him, a hand-lettered poster read ALL POWER TO THE PEOPLE! in bold black print.

"Tonight, we're going to talk about some of the things that are going on right now and what we can do as a community to make a difference. We're going to talk about the Black Panther Party and how you all can help my brothers here"—Leroy pointed to Stick and the others—"make Chicago a better city for black folks. It's time for a change, brothers and sisters." The crowd murmured. "We've been where we're at for too long. There's a time to sit still and a time to stand up. That time is now." The audience's rustling grew louder.

"Hold it down now, hold it down." Leroy patted his hands in the air to calm the class. "Now, white folks teach their children to be proud of their history and claim their future. The same white folks teach black children to be ashamed of their past, and that they have no future. The result is, the black man is trapped in the ghetto and his black children live in fear."

Leroy jumped off the desk and started pacing along the front of the room. "It's a hundred years since slavery and we ain't got nothing to show for it. If we wait for the government leaders to change their minds and their laws, we'll be waiting another hundred years. We don't need anyone's permission to be free."

He meant like the endless hours Father spent on making phone calls to lawyers and congressmen and mayors, all of them white.

"In order to change our future, we have to transform the present. You all know we are fighting a war. I'm not talking about the war in Vietnam, though that is certainly on all of our minds. I'm talking about the ways we fight right here on the streets in Chicago!"

Murmurs rippled through the crowd. People shifted in seats.

"I'm talking about the cops who beat down brothers for no reason except that they are black . . ."

The image of Bucky's face pressed against the sidewalk flashed in front of me. Maxie leaned her shoulder against me. Her fingers snaked between mine.

"I'm talking about the businesses that will not hire black workers, or give them equal pay. I'm talking about the ghettos that are crowded with poor black families. I'm talking about the jails that are full of black men . . ."

Around the room people nodded and clapped. Voices rose up.

"The time to change this country is now!" Leroy's words echoed over the restless stirring.

"That's right!" someone yelled. Everyone turned around to look at the guy who had shouted. He shrugged and sat down, looking a little embarrassed. A few people laughed. Some started clapping.

Leroy looked to the right and motioned to a man standing against the wall. He nodded, and the man stood up to attention. Leroy stuck out his hand. The man pulled a large black rifle from behind a chair and tossed it to Leroy. The *clap* of his hand against the barrel echoed in the air. The room fell dead silent.

"The revolution is not here," Leroy said, holding the gun aloft. "It's here." He tapped his temple with his free hand.

I got chills. People leaned forward, eyes fixed on Leroy.

"We will ensure our freedom by any means necessary, but before we can go here"—he shook the gun—"that freedom has to live here"—he pointed to his head—"and here"—he pointed to his chest.

Leroy walked the gun back over to the wall. My heart beat fast. Maxie's eyes looked as wide as mine felt. Leroy talked about the system of government, rules and law. He spoke of rights and privilege, the division between rich and poor. Father also talked about these things, but hearing it now, it all seemed brand new. And not just new, but possible. Leroy explained the Panthers' ten-point plan to achieve justice, and handed out a list of books we should read.

Then, Leroy stopped speaking. We all waited. He looked over the faces in the crowd, as if trying to decide whether or not to continue. He glanced at the row of bereted guys standing at the side. One of them, Lester Burns, nodded slightly.

Leroy cleared his throat. "Some of you have come to me, concerned about the things that went down in Oakland a few days ago."

I looked at Maxie. I didn't know what he meant. She shrugged.

"For those of you who don't know," Leroy went on, "I'm talking about the murder of your brother and mine, Bobby Hutton, during a raid by the Oakland Police on the Black Panthers' Oakland headquarters." He paused as the crowd murmured surprise and confusion.

"Seventeen years old. Unarmed. Hit with tear gas. Shot twelve times after surrendering to police."

The whole room burst into a mess of voices. Leroy let it go. When the crowd settled, he spoke again.

"Bobby may be the first Panther to die in this fight, but he's not the first casualty of the race war. Just the latest. And he won't be the last to give his life for the cause of freedom.

"The police will lie, say he shot first, and the world will look the other way. This is what we're up against. This can't go on." Leroy slid his palms against each other as he looked around the room. "That's it for tonight. Sign-ups are at the left tables."

He threw his fist in the air. "All power to the people!"

"All power to the people," the crowd responded. Everyone jumped to their feet.

As class broke up, Maxie hurried toward the tables. Raheem sauntered over to me. He studied me up and down, like he was trying to figure me out. "You finally decided to come, eh?" He hung his arm across my shoulders. "So, what'd you think? What'd you learn?" He grinned. Was he being serious, expecting me to answer?

"He really knows what he's talking about," I said, nodding at Leroy.

"Leroy knows where it's at, for sure," he said. He leaned

in closer to my ear. "But you got to wait till you hear Fred Hampton. That brother can talk you to tears."

"Yeah? Who is he?" I asked. Maxie moved forward in the breakfast sign-up line.

"He's the Chairman. He started this whole thing up here in Chicago. You keep coming out, he'll be here one of these times. See you next week?"

"Sure," I said. I had no idea what I was going to do ten minutes from now, let alone next week. I checked the clock. Nine o'clock! Mama was going to rip into me for sure.

Maxie was still moving from table to table, apparently signing up for everything. I'd have liked to walk her home, but I really needed to go. I waved to her and headed for the door.

"Sam," Stick called. I turned back. He walked toward me.

"What?" I tried not to sound hopeful. He wasn't going to say what I wanted him to.

Stick let out a long breath. "Nothing, really. I just wanted to say—good night."

"You know, you could come home with me," I said, unable to hold my tongue. Stick didn't bother to answer, he just looked at me. I couldn't meet his eyes. I didn't want him to know it was hard for me to stand alone. Stick had to be more alone than anyone.

"Sam, I can't compromise. Not on this. There's too much wrong." His gaze was so heavy, I could feel it pressing down on me.

I stepped closer to him, and he reached out and hugged me, tapping my back with his fist.

"I'll see you around."

"Yeah," I said, tamping down as much of my frustration as I could. "See you."

I slipped out the door, welcoming the cool air that brushed against me. A bit of the tension lifted off me, but not enough. I bent into the wind and headed home.

I felt all stirred up inside, so much that I couldn't make sense of my thoughts. I walked past the auto shop, trying not to look, but thoughts of Bucky filled my head. Bucky's smile, Bucky's blood. I turned onto Bryant Street, passed the spot where Bucky had fallen. I could still see him lying there. I hurried on.

I crossed the street to avoid the place where I'd stood when I heard about Dr. King, when the riots started. The images hurtled through my mind. The sounds. Glass breaking, the sizzle of flames, the whack of a nightstick.

I had to get off this street. I wanted to run, but I'd rather be in trouble with Mama than in jail. The cops see a brother running at night, they pick him up for sure. I didn't need a meeting to teach me that.

It wasn't much farther to the end of the street. I let out my breath as I turned the corner—and came face-to-face with Father.

He stopped short. "Sam?"

I ran up and wrapped my arms around him like I was five years old. Father touched my back lightly. His fingers moved over me as if he were checking for broken bones.

"What are you doing here?" he said over my head. His voice sounded strange. Not angry, or sad, or disappointed, not even surprised, just—blank. His hands folded over my shoulders.

I stepped away, feeling stupid for being so afraid. His eyes searched my face. What should I say? "Uh, my friend Maxie, she lives—"

"Sam, it's nine o'clock. Your mother must be out of her mind over you."

"She knows I'm here. I told her where I was going." It was technically true.

Father wrapped his arms around his chest. "She let you go out after dark?"

"It wasn't dark when I left." That was stretching it.

He drew in a shaky breath. "Come on, let's get you home."

The car was parked a couple of blocks away, very close to where the meeting had just taken place. I couldn't let myself bask in the relief of having Father to walk with me; it was overshadowed by the fear that we might run into Stick. I didn't know what would happen then. My world had been fractured enough already—it hurt to wonder what more might happen. Father usually knew how to fix things, but he wasn't himself lately. Even now, his silence frightened me. No lecture. Barely a reaction to my being out when I wasn't supposed to be. I didn't recognize this sad, quiet version of my father. He seemed deflated of the energy that had always defined him. He unlocked the car door for me and opened it. I looked at his face then, and something deep, so deep inside me shattered into a thousand pieces.

What would have been a twenty-minute walk took just a few minutes in the car. We drove in silence most of the way home, Father glancing at me from time to time. "What do you have there?" he asked, pointing to the papers in my hands.

I pulled the Panther information closer to my chest. "Homework."

Father regarded me out of the corner of his eye. "And you have it with you?"

"Maxie needed some help with math, so I came and showed her." Why did I have to lie? The shards already loose in me dug deeper.

Father nodded, steering the car into our driveway. "I

don't want you out after dark, Sam," he said as we walked to the door. "Straight home from school tomorrow. No detours. No outings, you hear?"

The reprimand lifted my spirits some, made me feel more normal. But I couldn't come straight home tomorrow.

"Samuel."

"Yes, I hear."

He opened the door and motioned me inside.

Mama leaped out of her chair and flew across the room as we came in. "Samuel Childs, where on earth have you been? You won't leave this house for a month, so help me. Where have you been? Answer me. Answer me!" I didn't have a chance to speak. She pulled me down and hugged me to her. I rested my head on her shoulder for a second, then straightened up.

"Sam, go to your room," Father said. I started to move away.

Mama pointed her finger at me. "Don't even think about leaving this room without explaining yourself."

"Marjorie—"

"Roland." Mama was too mad to speak further. Her mouth moved silently. She planted her hands on her hips and glared at Father. He stood very still, returning her gaze.

"Sam, give your mother and me five minutes," he finally said. I didn't need to be told twice. I spun around and went toward my room. "But we aren't finished here," Father called after me.

They waited in silence until I had closed the door behind me. Not that it mattered. Moments later, their voices drifted through the walls.

"What were you thinking, letting him go out at night?" Father said. I groaned and flopped down onto my bed. I glanced at the open window, but it'd be worse if I snuck out again. Much, much worse. I crawled to the end of the bed, near the block tower, and closed my eyes, longing to be engulfed in the magic protection of its walls. But my imagination betrayed me. I could only picture the gun, the block tower's magic destroyed by foreign invasion.

"I didn't *let* him anything, Roland. Where did you find him?"

"Bryant Street."

"I see. And where was he before that?"

"Doing homework with Maxie. I'd rather he bring her over here. It's not safe for him to be —"

Mama laughed. The gently musical sound echoed eerily down the hallway. "You need to open your eyes, honey."

Silence, long and heavy. I came off my bed and opened the door.

"He said he was with Maxie. Sam doesn't lie." I felt sick to my stomach.

"I suppose he doesn't sneak out the window after I've told him he can't go out either."

"What?"

"You heard me."

"Get him out here. I'll talk to him."

"And say what?" Mama sighed. "Never mind, you always think of something."

"What's that supposed to mean?"

I sat on the floor in the hall and leaned against the doorjamb, practically holding my breath. I hugged my knees to my chest. I could count on one hand the number of times I'd heard my parents fight. They disagreed, they discussed, they debated, they retreated to their bedroom to hash out their differences out of my earshot. But fight? Almost never. Definitely never over me.

"You're missing the point, Roland. This is Sam we're talking about. Sam. We're losing him, too." Her voice shook with anger and fear. I rested my head on my knees.

"Sam is not Steve," Father said.

"How do you think it occurred to him to go out the window?"

"Sam's different. He is not going to—"

"What would you have done at his age?"

The floorboards creaked as Father began to pace. Back and forth in front of the windows, the way he did when searching for inspiration for one of his speeches.

"My situation was totally different. The first demonstration I attended was in law school."

Mama stamped her foot. "Forget the demonstration. Forget the world for a minute. Look me in the eye and tell me what I can say to our sons to give them hope."

Father spoke quietly. "I feel their pain, Marjorie—why do you think I'm doing what I do?" He rarely used this low tone of voice, and it meant he was out-of-his-mind furious. The angrier he got, the steadier his voice became, until it seemed as if he were speaking words etched in stone.

Mama's words, in contrast, were sharp and clear, sliding like daggers from her tongue. "While you are thinking about the community, the city, the country, I think about this family. I don't care what you say from behind the podium, but you can't walk in that room with more of the same.

"It was easy when they were little. When they looked up at you. You might as well have been God to them then. But they're not little anymore. They're finding their own ways now, and finding truths other places than in you."

Father's pacing stopped. "I don't have to listen to this."

"No, you don't." Mama laughed again, but not happily. "Close your ears and open your mouth like you always do."

"Marjorie—"

"It's okay, though. I don't need to be heard. They do."

Silence. So much silence, I fought the urge to go out and make sure everyone was still breathing in the other room.

"I'm going for a drive," Father finally said. "Don't look at me like that. You don't want me to talk to Sam. What am I supposed to do?"

Silence. I pictured them staring each other down as they had when Father and I had first walked in.

"Drive then," Mama said. "Just know that you're going to end up right back here with me, with Sam, with all the same problems in front of you. You'll have to deal with us sooner or later. Not talk to us. Deal with us."

"Fine. I'll stay and we can argue some more."

"Let's." Mama came around the corner. She stopped short when she saw me sitting there. "Samuel, get in here," she said, as if I hadn't heard the entire conversation.

I trudged back to the living room, feeling as though I were headed for the guillotine. If it always felt this way to break rules and get caught, I was better off being good.

"Explain what happened tonight," she said. "Pick up your head and look at me."

"Yes, Mama." I breathed deeply and looked in her eyes. I couldn't lie to her. She knew. Somehow, she already knew. "I went to a political education class."

"What were you thinking?" Father's granite demand

placed the last straw on the load I was carrying.

I spun toward him. "What do you want from me?" I shouted.

Father's stunned expression sucked the fight out of me. I'd never talked back to him. Never. He gazed at me with slack-jawed incredulity. I had shocked him into silence, and that was saying something.

"Sam," Mama said sharply.

I lowered my gaze to the carpet. It swam in front of my eyes. "I had to go, Mama."

Her tone softened. "Tell me why, baby."

Why? If only I could explain it, what it felt like to run in place, to see the same things day after day and not be able to do anything about them. How it felt to be alone in a dark room in the middle of the night, with a gun in the tower and the whisper of wind through the always-open window, knowing there was nowhere else for me to be.

Father and Mama were expecting me to speak. She nodded gently, and I knew I had to try to say something out loud.

"I—I wanted to know what it would be like. And—and Maxie was going. Everything's real bad right now, and I wanted to see Stick. I wanted to see if there's something I can do."

"Are you hearing this, Roland?"

He nodded curtly. "You've made your point. Let's move on."

"Move on to what?" I cried. "So you know where I went. So I'm grounded. So what? It doesn't change anything."

"There's a lot you can do, son. Bucky's trial starts next week. You know we're holding a demonstration."

I nodded.

"There's a lot to be done before then, though. You can help me." He cleared his throat. "I'd like it if you'd help me."

"All right," I said, too tired to protest. Bucky's face floated in front of me. But thoughts of him always ended on the pavement, with a thwack, a cry, and the churning of my stomach.

Father sank down onto the couch, resting his elbows on his knees and rubbing his forehead. I stood beside the couch, waiting. When he raised his eyes to me, he looked so drained, as if he didn't even have the energy to be upset with me. I could see his sadness, sense that something was broken in him, too. "Get to sleep, Sam. You have school tomorrow."

I started toward my room.

"Sam." I turned back. "No more talk about the Black Panthers, is that clear?"

I hesitated. "Yes."

"I need you to stay away from them."

"Good night," I said, and headed to my room. I closed the door behind me and stood in the center of the room, looking around as if I hadn't spent every night of my life in this space. My gaze fell on the block tower. I lunged for it, tugging away blocks so hard, the small section of wall tumbled to the floor. My hands trembled as I withdrew the gun. The cold weight of it startled me, and I let it fall to the carpet. I wrapped it in one of Stick's shirts.

I took a shoe box from the closet and stuffed the gun and shirt inside, then glanced around the room. I shoved aside a stack of books underneath my bed and pushed the box up against the wall, hidden from view. Then I rebuilt the tower, smoothly aligning its walls to toughen it against future invasions.

I lay in bed, reading the papers I'd picked up at the meeting. One was the Panthers' newsletter from Oakland. The front-page article was all about that kid Leroy had spoken about, Bobby Hutton. The one who died in Oakland, surrendering to the police. He was the same age as Stick. The article said he hadn't done anything. Just ended up in the wrong place at the wrong time with the wrong color skin. Like Bucky.

I pushed the papers away and they floated to the floor.

Too much was happening too fast. Nothing seemed right anymore.

I tucked the covers tighter around me. Stick's vacant bed seemed bigger, emptier than ever. For the first time, I understood that he really might not be coming home.

CHAPTER 9

WHEN I WALKED OUT OF SCHOOL the next day, Maxie was waiting for me. The schoolyard noise and chatter around us seemed louder than ever. The world suddenly felt so much bigger than the two of us.

"I missed you at breakfast," Maxie said. "The meeting was incredible last night, wasn't it?" Her eyes shone as she gazed up at me. She grabbed my hand.

"Yeah," I said, forcing a smile. "Pretty amazing." I'd barely slept all night, for thinking about everything that was happening. I was more confused than I'd ever been.

"Ready to go?" Maxie tugged my hand.

I pulled my fingers free. I hated to do it, but I had no choice. About anything, it seemed. "I can't walk with you today."

"Why not?" Her eyebrows dropped into a V when she frowned.

"I'm in trouble. I have to go straight home."

Maxie moved closer to me. "What happened?"

I stepped back. "My dad found out."

"What did he say?" She tipped her head back, gazing at me so openly that I longed to pour the truth right into her. I wanted to hug her close and tell her everything. She could take it. Looking at her, I knew she could carry the weight of the world and still walk tall. It was me who was weak.

"I can't really go into it right now. I'll see you tomorrow, okay?"

"Tomorrow, then." Maxie smiled, but the light didn't reach her eyes as they searched my face.

"Sure," I said, moving away.

"Sam?" Maxie called. She motioned me back. "Is everything okay?"

"Fine." I kissed her cheek. My lips held on as long as I could let them. Maxie fixed her deep gaze on me. She didn't believe me. I walked away quickly, before I had to lie to her again.

Father was waiting when I got home. He sat in his usual place at the dining table, the phone against his ear, with the cord stretching behind him from the kitchen. He glanced over when I came in and motioned me toward the couch.

I hung up my jacket and went to the couch, but I didn't sit down. The living room was strewn with books, papers, signs, and things in preparation for the demonstration Father would hold during Bucky's trial the following week.

I moved through the familiar clutter differently this time, as if I had never seen it before. It wasn't unusual—our house always came alive with protest paraphernalia in the weeks before a demonstration, but I had never really paid attention to it before. Sure, I'd painted my share of signs and stuffed enough envelopes that I was certain every part of my hands had been paper cut at one time or another. These things were a part of me, so much a part that I'd taken them for granted.

The whole room spoke of the movement. The story of Father's work, the work of so many others, spelled out on our walls. Their triumphs and failures, the soul they carried, the injustices they strove to change.

I went to Father's desk and gazed at the frames that filled the wall. Photos of demonstrations. Texts of speeches. Newspaper clippings that mentioned Father's name; the earliest ones, from back when seeing his name in print was a novelty. Mama still collected the news pieces, though there were now too many to have on display. My gaze landed briefly on the stack of clippings Mama kept atop Father's file cabinet, then I returned my attention to the wall.

I studied the photo of Father smiling, his arm around Dr. King's shoulders, shortly before the speeches began at the March on Washington. The steps of the Lincoln Memorial in the background, where Dr. King would deliver his famous speech. How strange that he would never speak anywhere again. I squinted at Mama's neat print along the matte of the frame: .

Roland Childs and Martin Luther King March on Washington for Jobs and Freedom August 28, 1963

"Do you remember that day?" Father asked softly. I hadn't heard him come up behind me. I dropped my gaze away from the photo, but something drew my attention back to it.

"You had just turned nine," he said.

I looked at Father's face in the picture as I answered.

"Some of it." The white steps. The people. The heat of the summer sun beating down. They all ran together in my head sometimes, all the different crowds. But that day had its own separate space in my mind. I had never seen so many people, or been so hot, or stood in one place for so long. I remembered the huge white monuments poking up above the heads around me.

Stick had lifted me up for a minute so I could look over the people next to us. All I saw was people, as far as I could see. I thought everyone in the world had come to Washington, that we were celebrating the end of all the protests. I couldn't imagine that there was anyone left in the world to hurt us.

Remembering the extreme joy I'd felt at that moment made the ache within me now seem ten thousand times worse. I crossed my arms over my stomach.

"Did you know that day that you were doing something famous? Something everybody would always remember?"

"Yes," Father said. "In his speech, Martin called it 'the greatest demonstration for freedom in the history of our nation.' Yes, we knew."

I nodded.

"It was just one of many powerful experiences we shared, but it's the one the world remembers.

"Planning it took everything out of us," Father said. "We were all so tired that day. Tired of marching, demonstrating, organizing. The whole thing."

I tilted my chin toward my shoulder so I could see him behind me. He stared at the photo, didn't acknowledge me at all as he spoke into his memory. The look in his eyes mirrored something I felt within me. His words filled me up just a little, knowing maybe I wasn't so alone.

"But something happens once you get out there," he said. "When you see the faces, their hope, their dedication. We left everything we had on those steps, but we took something away with us too. Something more valuable."

He blinked, like he was emerging from the photo back into the room. "Sam, our words and our bodies were all the weapons we had. But the whole country took notice."

He met my eyes, but I drew them away. I stepped around him and went to sit on the couch.

"People are more afraid of ideas than of guns," he said, with his back to me. "Don't forget that." He cleared his throat and began stacking papers on his desk.

"I'll need you to come straight home after school this week. This is a big one, and I'm going to need your help, all right?" He lifted the paperwork and carried it over to the coffee table without waiting for my answer. Did he really need my help, or was this just his way of keeping me off the street?

"What do you want me to do?" I asked.

He smiled, a glimpse of his usual self. I latched on to it, tightly as a life raft upon a churning ocean.

"I'll show you." He came over beside me, clapping his hand against my shoulder as he sat down. He seemed so pleased. I didn't want to let him down. And I wanted to do something for Bucky. This was better, anyway, wasn't it? Safe. Familiar.

Father and I worked for over two hours outlining the whole set up, pointing out problems and things we needed to do. He'd been doing it right in front of me my whole life, but I'd never fully realized how much work he did to get these demonstrations going. Now that he was trying to involve me, I started to see a whole other side of the movement. There were calls to make, letters to write, permits to secure, and other things I'd never thought of. I had a lot to learn.

The next day, I hurried out of school, hoping to avoid running into Maxie. The sky had clouded over and a light mist was falling as I left the building, but the rumbling in the sky hinted at a coming storm. I felt secretly grateful. Later, I could always tell Maxie that I'd rushed home because of the weather.

When I reached the steps, though, she was waiting. She stood leaning against the railing, one arm crossed over her stomach with the other elbow resting on it and her chin in her palm. She sighed when our eyes met, as if she'd been waiting all day for me.

The soft sound hit me like a fist in my stomach. I dropped

my gaze and walked past her without saying anything.

Halfway down the steps, she caught me. Her hand grasped my elbow. I shook my arm free, but her fingers closed around a handful of my jacket. I stopped. I had to.

I listened to the gentle whisper of her fingers against my sleeve. If I shook her off again, she'd let me go. That's how she was. But I didn't want to hurt her.

"What gives?" She stood two steps above me, so she could look me straight in the eye. I avoided her gaze, the hurt and confusion within it. She stepped down in front of me. She slid her arms under mine and rested her cheek against my chest like she was listening to my heartbeat. It touched me that she wanted to be close. But right then, I didn't have it in me to give her what she needed.

"Can we just walk, please?" I said.

We held hands and left the school. We walked slowly, in silence. I was grateful for Maxie's willingness to simply be with me and not to pry. It took us longer than usual to reach her neighborhood.

We passed the building where the Panthers held their political education classes. My grip on Maxie's hand tightened. She turned to me, questions in her eyes. She seemed so open, so ready. I had to tell her.

"Stick left."

More questions appeared in the arch of her eyebrows.

I explained what happened, about the fight and how Stick walked out.

"Wow," she said. "When?"

"Last week."

Maxie made me stop walking. "Last week? How come you didn't tell me?" She crossed her arms and stepped away from me. "I gotta go through a whole week getting nothing but grumbles out of you before you finally say what's going on?"

"I didn't think it was a big deal." Now I regretted telling her anything at all.

She kicked the curb. "You didn't think lying to me was a big deal?"

"I didn't lie."

She glared. "Well, you didn't say the truth, so it's the same."

"I'm sorry, okay? I thought — I guess I thought it would be over by now." A clump of grass poked out from a crack in the sidewalk. I trimmed it with my toe, then crammed it back into the crevice.

"What would?"

"You know," I said. "I thought he would come home. Put the Panther stuff behind him."

Maxie's eyes glowed. "You can't put it behind you so easy. We know that now."

I glanced away. "Maybe *you* know it."

Maxie moved around me. "What are you saying?" She tilted her head as if she was suddenly seeing me in a whole different light.

"I don't know, Maxie. My father says—" I paused.

Maxie planted her fists on her hips. "Says what?"

"He says we could get in a lot of trouble for getting involved with the Panthers."

Maxie snorted. "He should talk. He gets in trouble all the time. He's been arrested, been to jail, just like everybody else."

"It's different," I said. "Getting arrested for protesting—that's part of the movement."

"So are the Panthers. Except, they don't just march around and complain; they actually do things."

I searched for better words to say what I meant. "Father says the cops are out to get folks who act militant."

Maxie threw up her hands. "They're out to get all of us, Sam!"

"But when things are peaceful, it's obvious to everyone that the arrests are for no good reason."

"They don't need a reason. Maybe they do up where you live, but they sure don't down here."

"So, if they already come here for nothing, why go and rile them up with real reasons?"

"Like Bucky Willis gave them?"

I closed my eyes until the bombardment passed. Images of Bucky were never far from my mind. Every day they dug deeper, etched on my conscience, never to be erased.

"Shut up about that, Maxie. I was there too."

"And you still don't care?"

"Of course I do! I told my dad, didn't I? There's going to be a demonstration."

Maxie's eyes blazed, and she shook her head at me. "You still don't get it. Your dad and them, they took the cops' word over Bucky's from the start. You had to tell them the way it went down, and they almost didn't believe you. Nobody had to tell the Panthers."

I looked up and down the street. Maxie stood, fists clenched, in front of me.

"Maybe this is why I didn't tell you about Stick leaving," I said. "I knew you'd get mad."

"If you would have told me before, I wouldn't be mad now, would I?"

I rubbed my forehead. "I don't want to fight with you," I said. "I've got enough going on without us going at it too."

"We both do." She glanced down the street. "All right. I'm going home." She started walking. "I'll see you tomorrow morning."

When I didn't answer, she turned back. "You're coming to the breakfast."

I paused. "Let's just plan to meet after school."

"Sam—"

"I don't know, all right? I don't know."

Maxie tugged on the ends of her hair. "Breakfast never hurt anyone, best as I can tell."

"If my father finds out—" I shook my head. I didn't even want to think about what would happen.

"Who cares?"

"He's on my back all the time, okay? Mama never wants me to leave the house anymore. There's only me now."

"You gotta stand up for yourself, Sam."

"Look what happened with Stick. I can't get kicked out."

"You don't know what would happen."

"Oh, yeah? Let's see Raheem go tell your father about the Panthers and see what happens." Why did I say that? It was an empty argument. Maxie's father didn't even live with them.

"My daddy don't know which way's up," Maxie snapped. "And if he did, he wouldn't care what we do."

"Well, maybe if he did, you'd have a real life instead of being stuck up here in the ghetto." The words tumbled out of my mouth before I knew what I was saying.

Maxie took two steps back. Her lips parted and she blinked hard.

I crossed my arms and stared back at her. I tried to think of something to say, but I'd stepped so far into the wrong, I didn't know how to fix it.

Her eyes filled and she turned away. She walked down the street toward her building. I didn't try to follow her. Some things should never be said out loud, even if they're true.

CHAPTER 10

I WAITED UNTIL MAXIE DISAPPEARED INTO HER building. She never looked back. I didn't really expect her to.

The moment the door closed behind her, the misty rain grew more intense. Thick droplets fell, soaking my skin. I wondered if Maxie had some magic control over the weather, the ability to protect herself but dump on me. Apparently, I had the same ability with my words.

I headed for home. I was already wet and already late, so I didn't bother to hurry. I hated myself so much for what I'd said that I could hardly see straight. The rain wasn't helping my mood in any way. I only felt muckier—nothing was washed clean.

A car pulled up alongside me, slowing to match my pace.

Father. I didn't have to turn my head to know it was him. I recognized the engine's hum and caught a glimpse of the tan hood out the corner of my eye.

He tapped the horn, but I ignored him. I walked for a while longer with him rolling next to me. He finally leaned over and lowered the passenger window.

"Getting a little wet there, aren't you?" He spoke lightly, as if it were a regular day when everything was normal. I kept walking, hoping he wouldn't be able to tell that my face was wet with more than just rain.

"Sam, get in the car please."

"What's the point?" I spat.

"You seem to have gone a little out of your way."

I rubbed a layer of water off my mouth. "So you came to check up on me because I didn't come straight home?"

Father sighed. He stretched his arm along the back of the bench seat. "I came to offer you a ride because it's raining."

"I said I'm fine."

"Suit yourself." He sped up and passed me. At the corner he stopped and waited. He watched me go by. I shook my head. He drove on ahead.

He was sitting in the car when I walked up the driveway. He got out and we entered the house together.

Mama emerged from the hallway as we came in.

"Sam, you're soaked," she exclaimed. "Roland, you were supposed to pick him up."

Father hung up his coat and dried his hands on his pant leg. "Your son inherited your stubborn streak."

"Um-hmm," Mama said, raising an eyebrow. " 'Cause you're such a pushover yourself."

They laughed softly together. I didn't see what was the least bit funny. I ripped off my jacket and went to my bedroom. I put on fresh clothes, leaving the damp ones in a pile on the floor.

I started back to the living room, but changed my mind. When Father wanted me, he could come and get me. I sat on my bed and leaned against the pillow.

Maxie would never forgive me for saying what I had. She wouldn't want me around anymore, wouldn't push me to do Panther stuff with her. Maybe now I could return to Father's world, bring all of myself back to the place I'd started from. Maybe I could learn to ignore the gnawing in the pit of my stomach telling me it wasn't enough.

Rain pounded against the roof and windows, steady and low, drumbeats announcing the presence of the sky. The walls groaned back at the rustling wind. But the storm outside couldn't compare to the one in my head. I lay on my bed and stared upward, wishing I could make my mind as blank as the ceiling.

How could I want so many things that didn't match?

o   o   o

In the morning, even though it was Saturday, I tried to hurry out of the house. Despite wishing that I could just let her go, I wanted to make up with Maxie. I hoped I could catch her on her way to the breakfast.

Father stopped me in the hall. "I have a couple of new ideas for the demonstration that I'd like to discuss over breakfast." He gave me a pointed look. Had he known where I was going?

I spent the whole day working with him. Fred and Leon stopped by for a while, permits in hand, to discuss legal issues with Father. He knew the answers to every question they asked, and he only had to look up one thing in one of the thick books on his desk. I was pretty impressed.

In the afternoon we worked at the dining table typing letters and stuffing them into envelopes. I matched the letters Father had typed to each of the envelopes he was addressing. He stopped working and studied me like he was going to say something, then went back to the envelopes as soon as he saw me glance up.

"What is it?" I said. The silence between us was taking its toll on me, too.

He hesitated. "What would you be doing if you weren't helping me?"

It wasn't the question I was expecting. "Probably walking

somewhere with Maxie." I lied. I was sure she was still mad at me, and I couldn't blame her.

Father nodded. "She seems like a nice girl, Sam."

I stopped folding, recalling the night I'd brought her home. Father's eyes clouded. After a moment, he cleared his throat. "You can bring her over to help, if you like. I just don't want you hanging around in the street so much."

I drew my finger along the creases of a letter. "I'll tell her," I said. If she ever spoke to me again.

Several nights later, I lay staring alternately at the block tower and the bedroom ceiling, trying to think of how to say I'm sorry to Maxie. She hadn't spoken to me since our fight; she'd been avoiding me at school. The hurt look in her eyes haunted me. I didn't know how to take back what I'd said.

Tap, tap, tap. A sound at the window. I moved the curtain aside and looked out.

Stick stood there, leaning against the side of the house.

"What are you doing?" I said. "Come in." I raised the window.

"I can't."

I reached past the curtain and grabbed his shoulder, but he pulled away. There were red smudges on my fingertips.

"Stick, you're bleeding!"

"Shhh."

"Get in here," I said, lowering my voice.

"I don't think I can," he said.

My heart began to race. "What happened? Where are you hurt? Stick?" I leaned toward him so far I nearly fell out of the house. Stick braced his hand against my shoulder to stop me, grimacing as he moved.

"Be quiet and stop panicking. I'm fine."

"You are not." Stick must have climbed in and out of our window a hundred times. He could have done it in his sleep.

"It's just my ribs are sore. You got something I can step on?"

I dragged my desk chair to the window. "Stand back." I lowered it out the window, trying not to make too much racket.

Stick stepped on the chair and then turned and sat on the windowsill. He sat with his back to me for a moment.

"I've got you," I said. Stick leaned into my arms and I pulled him inside. He was too heavy for me to hold. I half tripped, half fell onto the carpet with him on top of me. I moved him to the side and sat up.

Stick's eyes were pinched shut, and he was hugging his chest. He lay still on the floor. Seeing him in the light, I gasped.

"Oh, my God." His eye and cheek were swollen and his lip split open.

"Would you hush?" he snapped.

I glanced toward the wall between the bedrooms. "Sorry." I got up and pulled the chair back inside, then closed the window. Stick touched his face and winced.

"Hold on." I stepped into the hallway, closing the door behind me. I listened for a moment. Father was in the living room and Mama was puttering around in their bedroom. I rushed to the bathroom and dampened a cloth from Mama's clean rags bin. I grabbed a dry one, too, and a couple of bandages, and carried them back to Stick. I closed and locked the bedroom door.

Stick was leaning against the side of his bed. I knelt beside him and used the wet cloth to wipe the blood off his face and neck. "What happened?"

He opened his uninjured eye and looked at me.

"Sam?" The doorknob creaked. "Why is this door locked?" Mama said.

Stick stared up at me with a panicked expression. He clutched his side and leaned toward the window.

"Quick," I whispered. I helped him to his feet and shoved him toward the closet. He dodged the block tower and slid inside.

"Sam?"

"Coming, Mama." I shut the closet door and tugged my shirt over my head. "I'm changing." I tossed the shirt under the desk and unbuttoned the top of my pants. I held on to them as I pulled the door open.

"I'm changing," I said again. I rebuttoned my pants while Mama watched.

"Sam, what's on your pants?" Mama touched my leg above the knee. "Is that blood?"

"Oh, yeah. Paper cut." I held up a finger. She studied my hand, so I lowered it. "You can't even see it anymore."

Mama surveyed the quarter-size stain, bigger than a paper cut should cause. "It must have been deep. You need a bandage?"

"No, it stopped bleeding."

She handed me an armful of clean clothes. "You'll need these tomorrow. Now, get those pants off and I'll put them to soak."

"Okay, Mama." I half closed the door and stood behind it. I tugged off my pants and slid into my pajamas. Mama stepped in and picked up my dirty pants from the floor.

"It's getting late, Sam. Put your light out and go to sleep." She draped my pants over her arm and glanced around the room. Her eyes lingered on Stick's neatly made bed. After a long moment she kissed my forehead and went back into the hall. "Sleep well."

"Good night," I said, pushing the door shut. I listened until her footsteps moved down the hall, then I turned to the closet.

Stick was huddled up in the corner, his head resting on his knees. I touched his shoulder. "It's okay," I said.

Stick lifted his head. His eyes were cloudy and half closed, his cheeks damp. "I have to go."

"You ought to sleep here," I said. "I can lock the door again."

"No," he said. "I have to go." But he dropped his head back to his knees.

"Come on," I said, helping him up. "Don't be ridiculous." He leaned against me as we walked slowly back to his bed. I pulled back the covers and he sat down. He looked up at me and I nodded. "Stay."

Stick started to bend forward but sat up, clutching his chest. He hissed through his teeth for a couple of breaths. "Damn."

"What is it?" I said, leaning over. "Let me see." I tried to pull his shirt up.

"No." He batted my hands away. "I'm fine. Just get my shoes." I knelt in front of him and took off his shoes.

"You want pajamas?"

He shook his head. "She'd notice that." He tucked his legs under the covers and lay down. He closed his eyes and breathed deeply, wincing a little as his ribs expanded.

"Where have you been staying?" I knew he heard me, because his forehead wrinkled, but he didn't answer. I didn't want to press the issue.

"Your hair is long," I said, patting his Afro.

A hint of a smile touched his lips. "Yeah."

"I'm glad you came back." I flicked the light off and locked the door. By the time I got into bed, Stick's breathing had smoothed out. I lay down, listening to the familiar sound. It was like coming home for me, too.

I was still asleep when Mama knocked on the door in the morning. I blinked into my pillowcase.

"I'm awake!" I called, my voice muffled by the sheets. The doorknob turned and the hinges creaked. I sprang up. "Don't come in, Mama!" I was sure I'd locked the door.

Mama frowned at me from the doorway. "Here are your towels," she said, laying them across the desk. "They're clean."

I looked toward Stick, but his bed was empty, the blankets tucked in and smoothed. He must have unlocked the door too.

"Thanks."

"You're running late," she said as she closed the door. "Get a move on."

therockandtheriver

163

I leapt out of bed and opened the closet door. No sign of him. Then I saw the note lying on top of my shoes. Six words in Stick's quick block scrawl:

WHERE IS IT? I NEED IT.

I crumpled the page and tossed it in the trash. Kneeling beside the bed, I moved my books aside and reached for the box.

I stared at the gun for a moment, then I closed the lid and pushed the box back under the bed. I got ready in a hurry and headed out the door.

CHAPTER 11

WHEN I GOT TO THE SCHOOLYARD, Stick wasn't there. I spotted Maxie sitting at one of the tables. I started toward her, but she saw me coming. She got up and hurried in the other direction. I almost went after her, but the look on her face let me know she didn't want anything to do with me. I still didn't know what to say to her, and the Stick situation was too big in my head today, anyway.

I walked over to Raheem, who was dishing out eggs to the line of kids at the table. Raheem watched Maxie rush out of the yard, then he looked me up and down. I didn't appreciate the once-over. I already knew I wasn't good enough. For Maxie, for the Panthers. Any of it.

"Where you been?"

I shrugged. "Around."

"Not around here, though," Raheem said.

"I'm looking for my brother."

"He ain't here."

"No kidding," I said, crossing my arms. I don't know how it happened, but I felt myself slipping away from the calm and controlled me into something unfamiliar. "You know where he is?"

"Yeah."

I fought the powerful urge to scream. I didn't have time to play games. Raheem kept scooping food onto plates. He scraped up the last serving and lifted foil off a second pan. The yellow eggs captured the morning sunlight. My stomach rumbled at the light, salty aroma.

"Where?" I said, focusing on the hunger to distract myself.

"What's up with you and Maxie?"

"Nothing." I looked at my shoes.

"Don't try to sell me 'nothing,'" Raheem said. "I ain't buying. What'd you do?"

My head snapped up. "She's the one who —"

Raheem fixed a glare on me so hard I stepped back.

"It was me," I said, holding up my hands.

"What'd you do?" he repeated.

"Doesn't matter. Anyway, it's none of your business." I wasn't a fool, even if I'd acted like it toward Maxie. Raheem would mess me up for sure if I repeated what I'd said. I was lucky Maxie hadn't told him, or I'd be on the ground already.

Raheem pointed his serving spoon at me. A tiny piece of egg flew off it and splattered my jacket. "You better fix it."

"How am I supposed to fix it? She won't even talk to me. You saw."

Raheem handed his spoon to the guy next to him and wiped his hands on a cloth. He dropped the cloth on the serving table, then turned to me.

"Can I tell you something, man?"

"You can tell me where to find my brother."

He motioned me closer. "You gotta come sit with me, 'cause this is heavy." He walked over to a table where four of the young children sat. Raheem tugged one of the little girls' braids. She grinned up at him, clutching the strand in her fist. I sat down beside him and he leaned in.

"When I go down on Wednesdays, I listen up, you know?"

I nodded, not sure where this was going, or what it had to do with Stick.

"I take notes and all that," Raheem went on, lowering his voice. He glanced at the school building, then pointed his thumb at it. "They taught me how to read and write in there, but they ain't given me nothing worth reading or writing down.

"Leroy gives me all these books to read," he continued, "talking about poor people and black people, talking about the problems we have and what we gotta do to make things better."

"I know. I got the reading list," I said.

Raheem looked around. "Can you just listen up? I'm trying to talk to you, man. This is deep."

"Sorry."

"Leroy says the worst thing is for someone to feel hopeless. But, that's what happens when you live where we live too long. You get so you can't see past where you're at, and you can't believe there's anything better for you. You with me?"

I nodded.

Raheem raised his eyes to the sky and back. He folded his hands on the tabletop and sat quietly for a moment.

"Whatever happened between you and Maxie messed with her head." Raheem speared me with a gaze more intense than any I'd ever seen out of him. "It's bringing her down, and I can't stand that, 'cause whatever else happens to me, I gotta make sure that girl doesn't spend the rest of her life in this ghetto." His eyes dug into me, and I had to look away.

Raheem cleared his throat. "It's hard, living down there, you know?" He looked me over. "I guess you don't know, being from up the hill and all. Maxie, she's still got the idea

that she can make it. I'm gonna make sure that she does."
He clapped me on the shoulder. "Even if it means patching
things up between her and the likes of you."

"She won't talk to me."

Raheem laughed. "You got a lot to learn about women,
man. You're the one who messed up, so that means you're
the one who has to fix it."

"I'll try."

"Don't try. Do." He stood up. "I gotta work."

That afternoon, I looked for Maxie in the yard when I
came out of school. She was nowhere to be seen. I asked
a couple of people if they had seen her.

"It looked like she had someplace to be," one girl said.
"She tore on outta here."

"Thanks," I said. I headed for Bryant Street.

A couple of cops walked ahead of me, so I slowed down.
They turned onto Maxie's street. I slowed down more. If I
didn't see another cop as long as I lived, it would be all right
with me.

I wasn't in a hurry to get to Maxie. I still didn't know
how to fix what I had done. I looked away from the cops as
I approached Maxie's building.

I stood at the door and pressed her buzzer, 602. After a
moment, I pressed it again. Nothing.

Two shrieking kids ran tearing out, and I caught the door. I went in. The hall stank of garbage, urine, and other thick smells I couldn't recognize. There was a second locked door and set of buzzers, so I pressed 602 and held it. Nothing. Then I noticed a bunch of loose wires poking out from the edges of the button plate. I turned around and went back outside.

The cops were still there, standing by this kid Charlie, who was holding a large box. One of the cops had his nightstick out and was digging around in Charlie's box.

I moved toward the sidewalk and looked up at Maxie's building. In one of the sixth-floor windows, the curtain was drawn back. She stood there, her palm against the glass, staring down at the street. I knew she saw me, because her hand slipped a little, then she moved back where I couldn't see her anymore.

I jumped at a loud crash behind me. Charlie leaned over his box as its contents tumbled onto the sidewalk. His eyes widened and he shook his head as the cop waved the nightstick at him like a scolding finger.

I held my breath. This could be Bucky all over again. I wanted to get out of there, but I couldn't move.

A car pulled around the corner, slowing as it approached. It stopped suddenly and four guys got out. I gasped. Raheem, Leroy, their friend Lester — and Stick!

Raheem had a rifle resting against his shoulder; Lester carried one in his hands. They walked up to the curb where the cops were standing with Charlie.

"What's the trouble here, gentlemen?" Leroy said, crossing his arms. He looked first at one cop, then the other. "Has this young man broken some law, caused some disturbance?"

The bearded cop eyed the two rifles warily. "Take it easy, boys. We're just having a little talk. No need to get riled up."

Leroy smiled. "Good. If we're just talking, why don't you go ahead and holster that nightstick?"

The cop glanced at his partner, then hooked his baton back onto his belt. He held up his hands. "All right, boys, you put those guns down, now. We don't need any more of this nonsense."

Leroy and the others stood without moving.

The cop's face turned red. He raised his fist at Leroy. "Do it now!"

Leroy shook his head. "I don't think we can do that, boys." He leaned on the last word. "See, as long as nobody's breaking any laws or causing any problems, there's no reason for you to hang around, is there?"

The cops glanced at each other. Then the bearded cop hitched his chin at his partner. "Let's go." He took a step closer to Leroy. "You'd better wipe that smile off your face. You'll be sorry you pulled this stunt. All of you."

"You'll be sorry if you don't get out of my face," Raheem said.

The cops backed away. The four Panthers watched as they walked down the street and disappeared around the corner.

I could feel the blood rushing through my body. Everyone else on the street watched in amazement too, as the cops slipped out of sight without another word.

The Panthers turned and walked back to the car. Leroy clapped Charlie on the shoulder as he passed.

"Take care, kid."

"Yeah. Thanks, Leroy."

As they neared the car, Stick looked across the street. Our eyes met, but he seemed to look right through me. His glance was empty, but I felt it, as surely as I'd felt the gun this morning. Now I knew why he needed it. Why he couldn't tuck it away and forget about it. Stick blinked, then slid inside the car. Leroy pulled off down the street.

I had to get to Maxie, had to tell her what just happened. I turned around, and there she was. Right in front of me.

Her eyes were deep pools of accusation.

I swallowed hard. "Hi, Maxie. I was looking for you," I said.

"I know."

"How do you know?"

"Raheem."

Over Maxie's shoulder, Leroy's car turned the corner, headed the opposite direction from the way the cops had gone. I watched until the taillights disappeared.

"Did you see what just happened?" They hadn't needed to fight, or even to talk too much. The guns had said it all.

Maxie nodded.

"What did you think of that?" My heart was still racing.

"Policing the police? We need that around here."

I nodded. "It worked. They left."

"Whatever gets it done." Maxie crossed her arms. "You wanted to say something?"

I glanced around, feeling uneasy to be standing on the street where we were. "Yeah, but can we walk a little, first?"

Maxie nodded. We made our way down toward the lakefront and sat on our usual bench.

"I just wanted to say I'm sorry about the other day. I don't want to fight with you. And, that thing I said at the end was stupid. I didn't mean it."

She looked at her hands. "It's okay. You were right, anyway."

"No, I wasn't," I said. "I was just—I don't even know where it came from."

"Forget it." Maxie stood up. "Was that all?" She started to walk away. But something was still not right.

"Maxie? Where are you going?"

She turned around, fists on her hips. "Home."

"I thought we could talk some more. Are you still mad?"

Maxie tapped her toe. "I thought you were different. I thought where we lived didn't matter. I thought who our fathers are—or aren't—didn't matter."

"I didn't mean to say that."

"It's not that you said it. I care that you even thought it."

"I was just mad."

"Can't you see how that's worse?"

I pushed my hands into my pockets. "What do you want me to do?"

She stared at me, her eyes deeper than the lake beside us. "You worry that when people look at you, they see your father, right?"

I nodded.

"It's the same for me. People look at someone, they see what's messed up about their life, not what's good about it." She put her hand against my chest. "I thought we weren't like that."

"What do you want me to do?" I said again.

She stood quietly in front of me for a few moments, then she dropped her hand from my chest and stepped back. By the look in her eyes, I knew I had ruined everything.

"Can I walk you home at least?"

"I'm not really going home," she said. "I have stuff to do."

"What stuff?"

"Panther stuff. You wouldn't understand." She flipped her hair back. "You're over it, right?"

"I do understand," I said. "It's just—"

"Right, well, I guess I'll see you," she said, moving away.

"We're marching for Bucky tomorrow. I was hoping you'd come."

Maxie turned back.

"Not for me," I added. "For Bucky."

Something flickered in her eyes. "I'll be there." Then she walked away.

My mind raced as I made my way home. I thought about Maxie, how she was able to throw herself so completely into things, how she didn't seem confused. And I thought about Stick. Stick, who was so sure of everything too, while I didn't know anything at all.

The house was quiet when I entered. Father was not here yet with directives for today, so I went to my bedroom.

I pushed open the door, and there was Stick, rifling through my dresser drawers. He jerked his head up, startled. When he saw that it was just me, he resumed his digging.

"Hey!" I said. "What do you think you're doing?"

"I told you, I need it back." He slammed the last drawer shut and dropped to his knees between the beds. He started moving aside my books. I jumped onto my bed, flopping a lot so that he had to draw back his arm to avoid getting squished by the mattress.

"It's not here."

Stick straightened up and whipped toward me. "What did you do?"

"You won't find it." My pulse sped up. I couldn't let him find it.

"Sam, I'm not messing around."

"Me either."

Stick advanced toward me, with a menacing scowl. He grabbed a handful of my shirt and hauled me to my feet.

"You can't scare me," I said, but my heart was pounding.

"Don't bet on it."

"I'll never tell you."

He pushed me away so hard, I stumbled back toward

the window. "I don't have time for this," he said.

I rushed back toward him, pushing him as hard as he'd pushed me. "Good." I shoved him again, toward the door. "Go. Without your stupid gun."

"Stop it." Stick fended off my hands with a sweeping arc of one arm. The other hand he planted on my chest, keeping me at a distance. He used to do that when we were little and fighting because he was bigger and his arms were so long that I could kick and hit and only catch air. He used to laugh at me, flailing in front of him.

So, I did what I would have done then. I swung my foot. It connected with his shin.

"I know," he said, his eyes narrowing, "that you didn't just kick me."

"So what if I did?" My breaths came quick and shallow. Where were we going with this? It always had been a game, back then. I didn't know what it was now. Stick's hand was tight against my chest.

"Then you're toast."

He dove at me and we rolled to the ground. We'd fought before, but always in fun. This was different. Something real was at stake. We tumbled on the ground, no punches, just thrashing arms and legs and trying to get on top.

"Where is it?" he grunted, once he pinned me down.

"Not telling." I pressed upward, flipped, and wriggled

until the balance was off again. I thought I had a chance to get him, for once. Only because he'd been injured was I even able to match him.

Stick threw his weight and I kicked my feet at his, trying to flip myself on top. I missed. My right foot caught the block tower right in its base. I felt my shoe pass through the foundation. Blocks rained down on my leg.

"No, stop," I yelled at Stick, but we were locked in it. Stick tried to stop it too—I was sure that's what he was doing—but his foot followed mine, arcing across the face of the tower. More of it caved in, spilling around us.

"Sam?"

Stick and I froze.

"What's going on?" Father's voice boomed in the hallway. Stick and I broke apart. We leapt onto our respective beds, catching our breath.

Father appeared in the doorway. He glanced between us. A wave of emotions arced across his face. Anger. Frustration. Relief.

"Steven."

Stick stood up. "Father." They stared at each other for a long time. I stood aside, afraid to move or speak against the fragile balance in the air. Had Stick grown taller? His eyes gained power? He seemed as big as Father, and as strong.

"I have to go," Stick said. He stormed toward the door.

Father's arm shot out, caught Stick around the waist.

"Not so fast."

Stick stepped away, tugging the lines of his jacket back into place. "It's the job," he said quietly. "I'm not going to blow this."

Father laced his fingers together in front of his chest, then tapped his lips with his knuckles. "I know you won't," he said. He stepped out of the doorway.

Stick nodded. But he didn't move right away.

"How are you, son?"

Stick sagged a little, then drew himself up. "You don't have to worry about me. I'm fine." He glared over his shoulder at me, then swept past Father out the door.

"Why did you just let him go?" I stood up, too.

"If locking you two in this room for the rest of your lives would help anything, believe me . . ." He shook his head, like I should understand.

We looked at the block tower wreckage. It made me want to cry. The whole front part had collapsed, about a third of the whole. The remainder hung on precariously. I wished I could say the same for the hope inside of me.

Father cleared his throat. He probably guessed what had happened, but he didn't comment. "Let's get to work," he said.

I followed him into the hallway. In the moments it took

us to get to the living room, I wanted to tell him everything. Tell him about the fight. About the gun. Get it out of my room, out of my mind forever. Father would take it away so Stick would never get it back and I wouldn't have to worry about what he might do.

Instead, I sat down on the sofa beside a stack of demonstration posters. And I didn't say a word.

CHAPTER 12

WHE MORNING OF THE DEMON-
stration the sky dawned pale blue,
with easy rolling clouds. Father was
rather cheerful as he looked out the
front window at the perfect weather. "Should be a good
turnout today," he said.

I didn't care if it poured. For the first time, Father was
letting me stay out of school to go to the protest.

"Go on and get ready, Sam. We'll need to leave in a few
minutes to get over to the courthouse by eight."

I dressed in good pants and a button-down shirt.
Father said it was important to look like I meant business,
especially now that I'd be standing at the front with him.
I hoped a lot of people would come. Bucky needed all the
help he could get. I wondered if Maxie would really show
up. What would she think when she saw me up front, all
important-looking? Would she see then that I was trying?

Would she like me again, even just a little bit?

"You wouldn't understand." Maxie's words floated back to me. "You're over it, right?"

I'd said I was. Why couldn't she see past my words?

I reached under my bed for the shoe box. The thought of going to the march set my heart racing with excitement. But its beating held a twinge of fear, as well. What if Stick came back while I was gone? What if he found the gun?

I set the box on my nightstand. Now what? Anywhere in the room I put it, Stick might look. The dresser. The desk. The closet. Back under the bed. No good.

I flipped open the box lid and lifted the gun out. My heart raced as my fingers curved around the handle, slid into the grooves made for them. My index finger tucked itself around the trigger. I'd never held a gun before, and once it was in my hand, I didn't know what to do with it.

There was a round part in the center, and I knew that's where the bullets went. I pressed against the side, like I'd seen people do on television, and the barrel dropped open. Six silver slots, lying side by side in a circle, all empty. A stab of annoyance, or maybe disappointment, shot through me.

But I didn't want bullets. I didn't even want the gun.

"You wouldn't understand." Her words burned in my head.

It didn't matter what she thought. I knew I should go to the demonstration and stand by Father. That was the right thing to do. Wasn't it? For a split second, I wasn't sure.

I clicked the gun barrel back into place. Maybe if I just showed it to Maxie, just for a minute, she'd see there was more to me than—

"Sam?" Father knocked on the door, then opened it. I spun around, hiding the gun behind me. "You about ready?"

"I'll be out in just a few minutes."

"We don't have a few minutes," Father said. "We can't be late." He stood in the doorway watching me.

My hands had begun to sweat. The gun was slipping. I eased it into the waist of my pants, then moved my hands forward like I was adjusting my belt. My shirt was untucked, so I pulled it down to hide the gun.

"Let's go," Father said, waving me toward the door.

"All right."

I stepped forward, and the gun came with me. Just like that. Like it had always been there. The cold metal pressed against my skin. It wasn't a bad feeling. And this was one hiding place Stick would never think to look.

I glanced at myself in the mirror as I walked past Father and into the hallway.

It didn't show.

I'd never stood up front at one of Father's demon-strations before. Seeing the crowd from this side of the demon-stration was as foreign to me as seeing the earth from outer space. A sea of faces spread out in front of me, mostly black, but also a number of white, carrying signs and cheering for Bucky's release. In the front row a man stood with his tiny daughter perched on his shoulders. The girl held a hand-lettered FREE BUCKY poster that kept flapping in her father's face. His work-roughened hands wrapped around her pink shoes, anchoring her legs against his chest. Beside them, a balding man with hunched shoulders clutched the wooden police barricade for balance, swaying with the jostling crowd. I wondered if there had been this many people at the last demonstration I'd been at. The energy of the crowd thrilled me. I looked up at Father and smiled. He smiled back, patting my shoulder.

Buildings rose tall above the colorful cluster of heads and bodies. A totally different skyline view from the steps than from the street.

"Ready to go?" Father asked. I nodded, bringing my attention back to the crowd. Father stepped up to the micro-phone. He placed his hands along the sides of the podium, preparing to speak, but his face froze and he gripped the wood frame as if he needed it to hold himself up. I sucked in my breath and followed his gaze.

The Panthers had arrived. They marched in two straight lines right up to the courthouse steps. People moved out of the way to let them through. They looked so serious. The crowd's chanting faltered then stopped altogether as people turned to stare.

Leroy. Raheem. Stick. Lester. Charlie. Maxie. I did a double take. Maxie. She was dressed like the rest of them, black beret, black jacket, black shoes.

They stood at attention, right there in the center of the crowd. They didn't talk to anyone, or break ranks. They weren't there to start something. They were there for Bucky.

Father drew a long breath. He glanced at me out the corner of his eye, then began speaking. I wasn't hearing him. My eyes locked on the Panthers. I could've been down there with them. I could've been part of the reason everyone was staring. With Stick's gun tucked secretly under my dress clothes, I *was* one of them, wasn't I?

The crowd grew frenzied as the prison vans pulled up alongside the protesters. I gasped when I caught sight of Bucky. He looked thinner than ever, and he was built long and lean to begin with. They'd shaved his head smooth and dressed him in an orange prison jumpsuit. He was handcuffed.

Reporters leaped out of their vehicles, latched on to the small group, and followed Bucky into the building, shouting questions at him. He kept his eyes on the ground as the guards hustled him through the throng, up the courthouse steps, and into the building.

Shortly after Bucky arrived, the counterdemonstrators showed up. Forty or fifty whites, carrying posters and screaming at the top of their lungs. Their signs said COP KILLER and HANG HIM TODAY! Even though Bucky had done nothing to the cops who'd beaten him.

A line of cops streamed out of the courthouse and raced down the steps. They positioned themselves between our crowd and the angry white protestors on their way. I don't know what they thought they could do, but it didn't work. For a few minutes it was like watching oil and water: white folks on one side, blacks on the other. That didn't last long.

Father eyed the crowd from the podium. He resumed speaking. Against the rhythm of his voice, harsh cries rose from the edge of the crowd. The shouting, cursing, spitting sounds of the scuffle reached me all the way up front.

The Panthers broke ranks and filtered out through the crowd. Stick edged around people to get to the fighting, like a soldier looking for the front line.

A burly white man in a union jacket charged through

a line of people, fists flying. Stick intercepted him with a shoulder bump that sent the man reeling a few steps back. He caught his balance and lunged for Stick. Stick fought back, but his injury from two days ago hadn't healed. He wasn't hitting as hard or as fast as he could. He punched with his left fist, holding his right arm close to his chest.

The man slammed Stick in the ribs, then grabbed Stick around the neck and began choking him. Stick flailed his arms and tried to pull away, but he was in pain.

"Let go of him!" I screamed. "He's hurt!" My voice got lost in the noises of the crowd. I moved toward Stick.

"Sam!" Father stepped away from the podium and grabbed my shirt. "Sam, no!" I broke out of his grip and didn't look back. He called my name again as he plunged after me.

I dove through the crowd. I had to get to Stick. The crowd jostled and pushed me off course. They shoved me deeper into the center, past where Stick was. I turned around and fought my way back to him. Father made his way toward us from the podium. "Sam!" he shouted, drawing closer.

I reached Stick first. He was gasping in the large man's choke hold, his fingers pulling at the arm around his neck. My hands joined Stick's, tugging to loosen the man's grip.

The man released his other arm from Stick's waist and swung at me. He caught my cheek with his knuckles. The blow sent me reeling backward into the crowd. I fell hard. The gun jabbed into me, then slid out onto the ground. I rose up on my hands and knees, staring down at it. People jostled around me. Someone's foot clipped the edge of the gun, sending it skittering away. My hand shot out and caught it. I had to hide it again, before Father saw.

My fingers closed around the handle, and everything changed. I looked up at Stick, still struggling with the man, but I was no longer helpless. No longer did I have to stand by, watch, and wait.

Breathing hard, I lifted the gun from the pavement, stood up, and pointed it at the man choking Stick. "Let go!"

Stick flinched. A few yards away, Father froze. The man holding Stick stared at me with pungent hatred in his eyes.

"Let him go," I said again. The moment stretched out so long, I thought it would never end. I held my arm firm, but the gun was growing heavy.

The crowd parted, forming a little circle around the three of us. Father pushed into the opening.

"Sam." His voice was so low, I barely heard him.

The man looked at Father, then back at me. He slowly

withdrew his arm from around Stick's neck and stepped back. He melted into the crowd.

Stick stumbled forward. He came toward me, one hand on his neck, the other outstretched. "Give me the gun, Sam." He lifted it from my fingers. I was glad to let it go.

CHAPTER 13

STICK TURNED TOWARD FATHER, BUT I stared at the ground. I couldn't look at either of them. Someone grabbed me around the shoulders.

"Come on, kid." It was Leroy. He pushed me through the demonstrators, cops, and bystanders. Stick was right behind us.

We ran the few blocks to where Leroy's car was parked. I turned around and looked back at the crowd, but I couldn't see Father. He hadn't come after us—he'd let us go. Leroy nudged me toward the car. "Move it, kid! We can't hang around now."

Leroy got behind the wheel and hit the ignition. Stick shoved me into the backseat and eased in after me. His face was pale. He leaned forward and dropped the gun onto the front passenger seat, then turned to me.

"What were you thinking?" Stick demanded. He was

trembling, and he looked as though he might either explode or collapse.

Leroy put the gun inside the glove compartment. The latch closed, hiding it from view, but I felt as if I could still see it.

I didn't bother to answer Stick. What was I thinking? I couldn't begin to say. If I believed anything Father had ever taught me, I should've felt bad for what I had just done. Why didn't I? When Stick was in trouble, it didn't feel wrong.

"Are you all right?" I asked Stick. He leaned away from me with a sigh.

Leroy steered us away from the crowds, back toward the projects. "What's your name?" Leroy asked, looking at me in the rearview mirror.

"Sam."

"What were you doing with a gun?" Stick asked. "This was supposed to be a peaceful protest."

"You should talk."

Stick looked away.

"We can't win like that at this point, and you know it," Leroy said, frowning into the mirror. "Or, you should."

I stared at the rippling water as we drove along the lakefront. The wide calmness didn't match my mood, or soothe me. "None of this means anything anymore. You can scream till you're blue in the face, and still be standing in the same place," I said.

"They'll just learn to tune you out," Leroy finished for me.

I nodded. "Yeah."

I snuck a glance at Stick, but his attention was on the city, the walls and corners whizzing by his window. We were in the wrong seats. When we drove along the lake, Stick liked to sit where he could see the water, and me where I could see the buildings. But things like that didn't matter anymore.

Leroy parked near the building where they held the classes. The three of us got out and went inside to the meeting room. The space looked much larger with all the chairs folded against the walls. Two tables stood alone in the center of the room. Stick unfolded a chair and set it by a table. I sat down. Stick and Leroy pulled chairs up to the other table. I stretched my hands across the wood tabletop and rested my head on one arm. I didn't have the strength to ask what would happen now. Stick would know. Stick would take care of everything.

I sat up when Raheem and Lester thumped through the door. They both glanced at me warily as they walked in. I put my head back down and sat quietly while the others talked. I tried to listen, but all I could think of was Father. Father, and how I had shattered the sense of understanding we had built. But behind that thought, there was Stick. Stick, and how I couldn't stand by and let him be hurt. Which was worse? Hurting Stick by doing nothing, or hurting Father by doing what I did? My head ached with my thoughts, all the memories of moments I still didn't understand.

Leroy cleared his throat. "Whites are just beginning to recognize that equality really means they won't be on top anymore. There's a deep ravine between our races," he said. I got the feeling Leroy always did a lot of the talking and idea-making.

"Some of the whites who are supposedly on our side only stay there as long as our freedom doesn't interfere with their superiority. The hypocrisy is so deep, we can't even see it most of the time. And they never will see it." Leroy looked over at me. The others followed suit.

"So, kid, you ever been to the Wednesday political education class?" Lester asked. I almost laughed. How could he ask me that right now? It was such a normal question. But nothing could go back to normal after today.

"Yeah, one time," I said, sitting up.

Lester and Leroy exchanged a glance. "Why don't you come with us back to the office," Leroy said. "You can help us with —"

"No," Stick said out of nowhere.

"You saw what the kid did out there. That's what we need."

My heart surged with pride, drawing me back into the moment I'd pulled the gun. The thrill, the terror coursing through me. I'd done nothing with the gun but hold it in my hand, but for that one moment, I'd been heard.

Stick got up from the table. "Not Sam, Leroy."

"What's it to you?"

"He's my brother." I sat up straighter.

"I can see that. He looks just like you."

"He's too young," Stick said. What did Leroy want me to do? I wanted to know. I needed to know. I needed that feeling back, even for a moment—the sense that something I did made a difference.

"Well, you raised him right," Leroy said.

"I'm taking him home. Come on, Sam. Let's go."

"I want to stay," I said.

"You can't," Stick said.

Leroy rested his fist on Stick's shoulder. "You know it's not up to you. It's up to him."

"Let's go, Sam." Stick grabbed my arm and pulled me to my feet.

I yanked my arm loose. But Stick was still close, so close. I shoved him away. He staggered back, his thighs catching the rim of the table. His eyes flashed with a sheen of anger

keklamagoon

that frightened me more than a little. He steadied himself, clenching his fists, jaw tight as a cornerstone. I thought we were going to fight again. Right there, in front of everyone. But Stick checked himself, visibly tucked in his temper in favor of something else.

"We're going home," he said. "Right. Now."

I had no reins for my own frustration. My voice rose. "I'm not leaving."

Leroy's calm voice floated between us. "Listen, we've gotta roll. Why don't you two finish this on your way home? I'll catch both of you later."

Stick held up his hand and Leroy tossed him his car keys on his way out. The door closed with a thud, leaving us alone amid the sound reverberating off the concrete walls. Stick stalked toward me. "What are you trying to prove?"

"What are *you* trying to prove?" I shot back. "I can be brave too."

"You're not ready for this, Sam, if you think that's what it's about."

"Yes, I am. I'm going with them." I hurried to the door. But when I emerged onto the street, Leroy and the others were nowhere to be seen.

Stick came up behind me. "You're not ready for this life, so don't chase after it. You don't want it," he said. His tone was not mean, or even harsh, but I hated that he thought that about me. Even more, I hated that he was right. I didn't want to leave home. I didn't want to hold a gun. I had little voice left for protest. Mostly, I wanted to be left alone.

Stick went on. "This isn't something you ask for. It happens to you. I can't explain it. Someday something will happen and you'll know. Or it won't, and you'll live your life doing other things. It'll all be good, Sam."

I fought the powerful urge to storm off, but to where? Home to Father's lectures and disappointment? Following Leroy and the others toward . . . I didn't know what? I couldn't see how to move in either direction, but it hurt like hell standing still.

"Let's drive," Stick said, dangling Leroy's keys. We got in the car. I thought Stick would drive off right away, but instead he sat still for a while. He rubbed his forehead. "I never meant for you to get involved like this."

I crossed my arms. "Because you don't think I can handle it. Well, I can."

"Look, I never said you weren't brave," Stick said, softening his tone. "What you did today, that was brave. Brave and stupid." He swatted me on the back of the head. His hand bounced off the back of my hair. He smiled gently, a sad look in his eyes. "You don't always have to be like me."

I turned away, resting my forehead on the window

glass. "How can it be all right for you and not for me?" Down the sidewalk, two little boys tore after a rolling ball. Friends. Brothers, maybe.

Stick, too, watched the boys playing. "I don't want you to get hurt," he said softly. "I can't have that."

"What about you?"

"Keep coming to the meetings," he said. "Do the breakfast. And make up with your girl, because she's driving the rest of us crazy." He flashed a small grin, then became serious again. "Just leave the other stuff to me. I'm okay with whatever happens."

I sank down in my seat. I didn't like him saying that.

Stick slid the keys into the ignition.

"Wait," I said.

Stick paused, then shook his head. "I'm taking you home."

"No." I scrambled out of the car.

"Sam." Stick leaped out too.

I shut the door and looked across the roof at him. "I want to stay with you."

Stick laughed. "No, you don't. You're going back."

"I can't go home after what I did."

Stick studied the hood of the car. He ran his fingers along the metal fringe across the top of the door. "You can always go home," he said. "It's just not always easy."

"What am I supposed to say?"

Stick caught my eye. "You don't have to say anything. You won't be able to get a word in edgewise, anyway. Look, you've always been able to handle Father better than me. You're still the good son, Sam."

What was he talking about? There was nothing I could do better than Stick. Even if I could believe what he said, my actions today had surely ruined any favor Father may have felt for me. But what choice did I have? Run away, like Stick? Where did he sleep? What did he eat? Looking at him here, I still couldn't understand how he managed it. I wanted to go home.

We got back in the car. "Stick?"

"Hmm."

"I'm not sorry."

"I know," he said. "It's okay." Stick drove me home. He didn't say anything more, and I was too tired to try to talk.

"Come in with me," I said as he pulled into the driveway.

Stick braked the car and turned to me. He didn't reply, just brushed his thumb across his mouth in a move that reminded me of Father.

"I'll see you," I said. We clasped hands.

I waited until he drove away, then went inside. The

house was dark, but Mama was inside, watching television. An uneasy feeling churned up in my stomach. I glanced at the clock. It was barely afternoon. School should still be in session.

"I'm back," I said. "Mama?"

She didn't answer me. I went up beside her. Father was on television, getting interviewed by some reporters. "I maintain, violence is not the answer to these problems of race and discrimination. We must foster dialogue between the black and white extremes."

"Mama?" I waited for her to ask about the demonstration, but she didn't seem to notice me. She was sitting very still on the edge of the sofa, her handbag in her lap. I sat down beside her, and she jumped.

"Sam, baby." She ran her hand along the side of my face. "You're all right."

I lifted her fingers from my cheek and held them. "Mama, what is it?"

Father's voice shook with conviction that was discernable even through the television's fuzzy speakers. "We must come together at one table—the table of brotherhood, to use Dr. King's words—we must come together and hear each other out so that true justice and equality may—"

A scream erupted from the crowd on television.

The camera tilted, then righted itself. The familiar logo of a union jacket filled the frame. The man came out of nowhere, walked up to Father in broad daylight, big as life, and on television. And Father fell to the ground.

CHAPTER 14

WHAT HAPPENED?" I SAID, KNEELING in front of the screen.

"They're replaying it," Mama said.

"Why do they do that?"

I stared at the television. I couldn't see Father, but people in the crowd were screaming. They pressed closer, jostling the camera. Then the picture broke away and returned to a sound stage, where a reporter began droning. I listened, disbelieving. The man had had a knife, had stabbed Father, he said. His condition was unknown. The assailant had simply walked away in the confusion of the crowd. Hundreds of people around, dozens of police, and they let him walk away.

The law would not protect Father. They would always find a reason to strike down a black man, especially one with a sharp mind and a dangerous tongue. A man people listened to.

I touched the screen with my fingertips. Mama began to weep.

I went back to sit beside her. "Mama, we have to go to the hospital," I said. "Let's go."

"Your father has the car," she said, blotting her cheeks. "I thought you were with him. When I didn't see you there"—she motioned at the screen—"I thought . . ." She dissolved into tears again.

I put my hands on her shoulders. "I'm here, Mama. I'm fine. We have to go."

"Yes. We'll take the bus," she said. But she remained frozen in place, staring at the television. I brushed my hand over her hair. Mama was in no shape for public transportation, and I felt rather shaky myself.

"No, I'll find someone to drive us," I said.

I ran next door, but it didn't look like anyone was home. I banged on the door, anyway. No answer. Two doors down, no answer. Why should there be? It was the middle of the day in the middle of the week. I scanned the driveways along the street, then dashed across the road to a house with a car parked out front.

I pounded on the door, but no one came. A curtain fluttered, or maybe it was my imagination, but no one answered. I thought about going around back, but the sound of cars behind me made me stop.

Two media vans sped down the street, pulled up in front of our house. They took cameras from the back and went up onto our porch. I abandoned my search and ran home. I dodged the reporters, ducked beneath their cameras, ignoring the questions they fired at me. I slammed the door in their faces.

"Mama?"

She stood just inside the door, waiting with her purse in hand. "Who's here?" she said, looking over my shoulder. "Reporters?"

"No one's home. We have to ride the bus after all."

Mama went to the front window and looked out. A third press group had arrived. "No," she said. "They'll follow us." The bus stop was three blocks away, and who knew how long we'd have to wait there.

"So? We have to go."

"No." She glanced over her shoulder, a fierce protective light in her eyes. "I'm not taking you out there."

"But, Father—"

"Your father will be fine."

I walked toward her. "He will? Did someone call? From the hospital?"

"I know my husband," she said lifting her chin. "I know what he would want me to do."

o   o   o

therockandtheriver

The doorbell startled me. It had buzzed nonstop for the last hour, but each ring made me jump. I wouldn't answer. What did they want with us? Everyone knew Father's face, of course, knew what had happened. If I opened the door, we would be on the evening news. I didn't want Mama's tears on television. Every time the phone rang, someone wanted a statement. I took it off the hook.

There had been no word of Father since the television said they'd taken him away in the ambulance. I tried to call the hospital, but they wouldn't tell me anything over the phone. We had no car, no way to get there. Fred and Leon and Father's other friends had been out at the demonstration. I had no way to reach anyone, not even Stick.

Mama sat beside me on the sofa, clinging to my hand. She leaned her head on my shoulder. The television hummed, a jingly ad for laundry soap.

"I'm going to turn it off," I said, trying to pull away.

"We have to hear," she murmured. I got chills. She'd said those words before.

A key turned in the lock and the door swung open. The voices from outside grew louder. I turned around, my heart pounding.

Stick stepped into the hall. He gave me a long stare, and something tugged inside me.

"Let's go," he said.

Mama blinked at the sound of his voice, but she didn't raise her head.

"Stick's home, Mama," I said, shaking her off my shoulder. "He's come to get us."

We stepped outside, and my eyes opened wide. There was a whole line of brothers out there. Brothers in black leather jackets. Brothers with guns. They stood facing away from one another in two long rows stretching from the house to the street, where Leroy's car was waiting. I held Mama's hand as we walked.

The reporters were outside the rows of Panthers, photographing us and shouting questions, but they didn't try to break through. I ignored them, helping Mama into the backseat.

Father's friend Leon Betterly drove up and stopped behind Leroy's car. He looked at the Panthers, the reporters, then me. I climbed into Leroy's car beside Mama and closed the door.

The hospital corridor stretched, long and white, in front of me. It felt too familiar. Nothing but white, all around. There was no place for me to stand.

The day Stick got his head cut, I'd stood in this same room, with its uncomfortable rows of chairs and the bitter smell of blood and medicine mixing in the air. My head swam with the *swish-swish* of nurses' skirts as they hurried from room to room, and the *squeak-squeak* of gurney wheels echoing along the tile halls. It was the kind of waiting room that sucked away all hope, sent it swirling down a drain far out of reach. I felt as though I wasn't really there. I was someplace else.

Father's hand on my shoulder brought me back.

"What?" I said, blinking toward him. His face stood out, dark, against the waiting room walls.

"Are you all right?" he asked.

It wasn't Father, it was Stick. Everyone said they looked alike. I had never seen it for myself.

Stick led me to a seat beside Mama. His hand rested against my back as we walked, and I wondered where it came from, his ability to be strong and gentle at the same time. He sat down in the row of white chairs across from me. "They said he's stable. He'll be out of surgery soon."

"Praise the Lord," Leon said, raising his eyes to the ceiling.

Mama took my hands, and looked Stick straight in the eye. "It's those Panther kids that caused this," she said. "They've got everybody on edge."

Stick stood up and moved close to Mama. He touched the side of her face with the tips of his fingers, then, without a word, he walked away.

I couldn't let him leave that way. I placed Mama's hands back in her lap and followed Stick. He was standing by the window, apart from us. His hands were in his pockets, his back to the room.

I stood beside him. The wide blue of Lake Michigan stretched out in front of us. The color of the water blended with the sky at the horizon as if there was no opposite shore.

"He was just giving a speech," I said, closing my fist around a wad of curtain. I leaned my forehead against the cold glass. "It's so wrong."

"People like that guy don't know right from wrong," Stick said. "Just black from white."

"They think they're better for being white, but they're worse," I said. "I hate them all."

"No," Stick said. "Just the ones who do this."

"It's so messed up," I said. My eyes started to water, not from being sad, but from being mad. My head hurt, as if pieces of my brain had fallen out of place. I couldn't put them back. I couldn't put any of it back. Nothing I could do would fix what I'd made happen. "I don't know what to do," I whispered.

Stick nodded. He wasn't like Father. He wouldn't try to explain how I should feel or tell me what to think. Anyway, Stick knew all about being mad.

Leroy and Raheem stood near us. I hadn't noticed them come inside.

"We have to take off if we're going to make it before they wrap up for the day." Leroy said.

Stick went over and spoke quietly to Leroy. I strained to catch what they were saying.

"He needs to understand," Leroy said, looking at me.

"I'll meet you outside in a minute," Stick told him.

"I'm coming too," I said.

"No," Mama said, coming up behind me. "This family is broken bad enough." She glared at Raheem and Leroy, then turned her eyes on Stick.

"He's not going anywhere, Mama," Stick said. "Neither am I. I don't have to go anywhere."

Mama's voice rose. "You did this. And now you think you can walk back in and pick up the pieces?"

"Don't yell at him," I said.

Mama ignored me, focusing on Stick as she pointed down the hall with a shaking hand. "Your father got hurt without you by his side. He'll pick himself back up without you there, if that's what has to happen. But you are not going to take Sam away too."

"Stop it, Mama! It's not his fault. It's my fault." The words had been boiling inside me, filling me up. Now they were out, and I felt myself crumpling inward. "It's my fault."

My hands shook. I twisted up the curtain in my fingers and held on.

"Sam." Stick's hand on my arm. "Come sit down."

I couldn't breathe. Mama pushed Stick aside. She touched my face, my chest.

"Look what this is doing to your brother."

She didn't know. She didn't understand. "I did it! Tell her it was me," I screamed.

Stick watched me with an expression I'd never seen and didn't understand. I looked to Leroy. "Tell her!"

Leroy shrugged. "I don't see it that way."

"Enough," Mama said. "All of you, go."

Stick stuffed his hands in his pockets. "Mama."

"Go," she shouted. "Get on. Leave Sam alone!" She grabbed me around the neck and yanked my head down onto her chest, clutched me to her. Her chest heaved against my cheek, and the sound of her weeping cut into me. Her tears, heavy with fear, fell against my neck.

"Mama, let go," I said. She slowly withdrew her arms. I raised my head and kissed her cheek. "I love you, Mama."

Seeing her cry made my stomach ache. I didn't want to walk away.

I turned to follow Stick and the others. Leon Betterly stepped in front of me, said something to me, but I didn't hear him.

I rushed into the parking lot and stopped short. There was a whole crowd there, holding signs and candles and singing. It was as if half of Bucky's demonstration had shifted over a couple of blocks. People in the crowd tried to touch me as I passed, calling out good wishes. A tearful woman whispered, "We're praying for him," as her fingernails scratched against my sleeve.

Stick, Leroy and Raheem headed toward Leroy's car. I caught up with them at the edge of the parking lot. "You're wrong," I said, as I came up beside Leroy.

"Not often," he said, giving me half a smile.

"This wouldn't have happened if I hadn't—"

"Sam," he interrupted. He stopped walking and leaned toward me as if to hug me, but simply put his hand near the base of my neck and spoke into my ear. "You're only responsible for your own actions. You can't control how someone else reacts to what you do. You made a choice. Stand by it." He moved toward Stick and Raheem, who were waiting beside his car.

"I want to come with you," I said.

"Go back inside, Sam." Raheem put his hand on my shoulder. "You be with your mama right now. She needs you."

"Stick?" I said. His back was to me. "Stick, don't leave me here."

He didn't turn or even act like he'd heard me. He got into the car without a second glance. It was the worst thing he could have done to hurt me.

"Tomorrow," Raheem said. "He'll come get you in the morning."

They got in the car and drove off, leaving me standing alone. I didn't want to be there, didn't want to be anywhere except where they were going, but I couldn't follow. Even if I knew where to go, the part of me that was burned by Stick's betrayal wouldn't let me chase after him.

The crowd hummed a low, sad spiritual. I knew the words, but I didn't sing along. I waded through the soft-tugging rhythms of hope and desperation, and as I moved among the people, I couldn't help wondering, if Father wasn't there anymore, who would lead them? I erased the thought. Father would always be there. I pushed past everyone and returned to the waiting room.

CHAPTER 15

MAMA INSISTED ON SPENDING THE NIGHT in the hospital. No matter how I urged her, she refused to allow Leon Betterly to take her home or me to bring her anything to eat. She clutched my hand and wouldn't let go.

We sat in chairs overlooking the lake. I wished we could see the shore over the tops of the other buildings, to find comfort in the gentle surge of water onto the sand. But our view was of the lake's heart, where whitecapped waves churned in the deep. Each pocket of foam glowed pale in the moonlight as it surfaced, before the water's bulk swallowed it back down. The rocking water could not soothe my thoughts, but the feelings beating me up inside finally knocked me out. I sat feeling nothing but Mama's fingers pressing my palm, and my own pulse thumping beneath them. Everything else in me fell quiet. I wished for sleep, but it didn't come. There was nothing but the waves. The waves. The waves. Finally the gray light of morning touched the sky. The air began to blush with a hint of pink, streaks of red, orange, purple rising behind the water.

When it was finally, fully morning, the world looked right again. Except for the churning feeling I couldn't shake, that nothing could ever be the same.

The doctors let us in one at a time to see Father, who had come out of surgery back in the early evening. He was doing well, they said.

Mama went in first and came out looking refreshed. "He's going to be all right," she said, touching my arm. It was my turn.

There was a soft hum in the room, and the air smelled thick and warm. Father was lying on the bed, his eyes closed. The heart monitor beeped at the side of the bed, and two thin tubes snaked out of Father's arm, connecting him to an IV stand. I moved up beside him, quietly, in case he was sleeping.

His fingers brushed against my hand. "Sam," he murmured. I could barely hear him. "You're all right."

"I'm fine, Father. How do you feel?"

"Sore. Where's your brother?"

I have no idea. "He's safe," I said. "He was here with us yesterday. He brought us to the hospital."

Father's eyes closed. I thought he had fallen asleep, so I began to move away.

"You scared me," he said. I stepped closer.

"I'm sorry," I said. "I didn't mean for—" I choked on the words. My eyes began to ache, and I pressed my hands over them. I tried to concentrate on Leroy's words, but it didn't help. Father was lying there, hurt, because of me. "I'm sorry."

"Sit here," he said, smoothing his hand against the sheet at his side. I lifted his hand carefully and sat down. He ran his fingers over the sleeve of my shirt, then let his hand rest on top of mine as he drifted off to sleep. I sat there for a while, feeling his fingertips against the back of my hand. Letting the flutter of his eyelids tell me everything would be all right.

When I came out, Stick was leaning against the wall across the hallway. For the first time in a long while, I was not even a little bit happy to see him. I turned away from him for a moment while I rubbed my eyes.

"How is he?"

"You can go in if you want."

Stick shook his head. "He doesn't want to see me."

"He asked about you."

Stick pushed off the wall. "I came by to pick you up. Leroy's expecting you. Are you ready?"

I swallowed a surge of anger, but not all of it went down. "I was ready last night," I snapped. Why did he, too, think my life should run on his terms? I was old enough to make my own decisions.

"Do you want to come or not?"

"Tell me where and I'll get there myself."

"Don't be stubborn."

"It works for you. Where's Mama?"

"I asked Fred to take her home."

"How'd you manage that?" I said, but I didn't even care what he'd done. I already hated it, that he could come back and in a minute put right everything I couldn't manage in his absence. His shadow seemed as big as Father's, and I was lost in the whole mess of gray.

Stick started down the hall. "I thought I might have to carry her to the car. I can't believe you let her sit up all night."

Insult to injury. "She wouldn't have slept, anyway," I said.

Stick and I walked out to the parking lot. The vigil keepers had gone home, the only evidence of their presence was a few wax-stained signs strewn across the pavement.

Stick drove us away from the hospital, back down into the neighborhood. He stopped in front of a tall apartment building. He cut the engine and sat there for a moment. His fingers drummed lightly against the wheel.

"You look tired," he said.

"You would too, if you'd been sitting up all night." Stick did look exhausted, but I wouldn't give him the satisfaction of acknowledging it.

He nodded. "I could take you home, instead. They'll understand."

I opened the car door and got out without replying. Stick came around and led me into the building. I felt like a kid being walked to school. I glared at the back of Stick's head, wishing I could do this on my own.

The apartment was on the third floor, and we climbed the stairs quickly. Two guys I didn't recognize stood on the landing by the door, holding guns. I moved close behind Stick as he greeted them. One of them opened the door, and Stick motioned me through.

My gaze swept about the room, trying to absorb the sights. The apartment was cluttered with tables and chairs piled high with books and papers. The walls were plastered with posters and newspaper clippings and photographs, bombarding me with scenes from the life of the Panthers. Through a doorway ahead of me a second room appeared to contain more of the same. On the left wall, surrounding the windows, hung a huge curtain of African-print cloth. Deep blue swirled among lighter shades, like ocean draped in sky. The room had a voice of its own, a scream of outrage, a whisper of truth, and in the corner, a murmuring cry. I released my breath.

"Amazing, right?" Stick said in my ear. I couldn't answer him; I was busy drinking it all in, busy trying to understand the stirring in my chest. I'd never stood in this room before, but somehow, I recognized it.

Lester and Leroy were bent over a desk to my left, talking. They turned as we came in. I looked to the right, and Maxie was standing there. I stepped back, bumping into Stick.

"Hi, Sam," she said.

"Hi, Maxie."

She walked over. "I'm glad your dad is going to be okay." The bundle of dynamite burning in me suddenly diffused. She could do that somehow—melt me when I was cold, cool me when I was too hot to handle myself.

"Thanks."

She stepped up and put her arms around me. I didn't know what else to do, so I hugged her back. It only lasted a few moments. Then she moved away, sitting at a table with her back to me.

"Sam." Leroy greeted me with a bump of his fist against my shoulder. "You made it."

"I've got to get going," Stick said, moving to the door-way.

"You're leaving?" My heart sped up. If Stick left, I'd only be here because I wanted to be.

"Raheem took over the shift," Leroy said.

Stick turned, a flicker in his eyes. "I was going to cover it."

"You got bigger things today. Don't sweat it." Leroy went through the doorway to the second room, motioning Stick to follow. I started to go after them.

"Not so fast," Lester said from across the room. "We'll be needing you in here." He pointed me toward the desk where Maxie was sitting. I sat down in the chair she cleared off for me, but she didn't look at me or speak. She was tucking folded letters into envelopes one after the other and stacking them.

"What happens now?" I asked.

"Playtime's over, kid," Lester said. "We've got work to do. Help Maxie with the letters. We've got to get them out or we'll go broke."

"What are these for?" I took one of the letters off Maxie's stack and read through it. "Do a lot of people send in money?" I said.

"Something's got to pay for all that food you kids go through every morning," Lester said. "Not to mention Bucky's lawyers," he added.

"What?" I said. It had never occurred to me to wonder

how Bucky's lawyers were being paid for. He certainly couldn't afford them. But I never would have guessed the Panthers were behind it.

Lester just grunted at me. "Top drawer. Lick 'em and stick 'em." I pulled open the desk drawer. It was full of postage stamps. I took out a few sheets and began separating them.

Maxie met my eyes as she handed me a stack of stuffed envelopes.

"Where was Stick going before?" I asked, trying to make conversation.

She gave me a funny look, like I should already know. "Roy Dack's."

"The auto shop?"

Maxie nodded. "Someone's got to fill in for Bucky every shift or Roy's going to hire someone else to take his place. Someone who won't quit if—when Bucky comes back."

"Stick doesn't know about cars," I said. "Not like Bucky."

"He must have learned." Maxie handed me another stack, and we stopped talking to concentrate. I licked stamps and envelopes until my mouth went dry. I paused and spent a few moments rolling my tongue around my mouth, trying to bring life back to it.

Maxie snickered. "You can use the sponge, you know."

I glared at her. "Now you tell me. Where is it?"

"I left it in the kitchen." She grinned and angled her head toward the other room. "Through there."

I shot her one last dirty look as I walked into the other room. Stick and Leroy were sitting in low-backed armchairs facing a bookcase that filled one entire wall.

Stick rubbed his forehead and leaned back in his chair. "I'm saying, I don't think it's a good idea," he said.

"And I'm saying, you need to talk to Sam about it." Leroy drummed his fingers along the armrest.

"Talk to me about what?"

Stick sat up and turned. "Sam."

"Bucky's lawyers still want you to testify at the trial," Leroy said, tilting his head back toward me.

I went around in front of them. "Still? They never asked me."

"Father said no," Stick said quietly. "And they respect him too much to go against him."

Just like that, my fuse reignited. "Why didn't anyone tell me? Father wants me to help Bucky as much as I can! He said so."

"There were plenty of witnesses, Sam," Stick said, glancing at Leroy. "He didn't want you to get any more involved than necessary."

"But they still want me?"

Leroy leaned toward me. "You're Roland Childs's son. People know your name, and that means the jury might be more likely to believe your story."

"I'll testify," I said. "I saw what happened. Bucky doesn't deserve to go to jail."

A muscle in Stick's cheek twitched. Leroy smiled. "Good. Now you just have to convince your father."

"I don't need his permission, do I?"

"No," Stick said. "But if he asks them not to put you on the stand, they won't."

"Just to make him happy? Even if it's worse for Bucky?"

"It's more than that," Stick said. I waited for him to say more, hating the fact that I didn't know things.

Leroy brushed his hands together. "Well, my work here is done." He stood up and looked at Stick. "Help him figure out what to do to make this happen."

Stick nodded. Leroy pressed my shoulder as he passed. "Make me proud, kid."

Stick studied me for a few moments. "I know you'd do anything for Bucky," he said. "But this is a big step."

"I can handle it. Why don't you want me to?" Finally, something I could do that Father and Stick could not. I was determined to be there for Bucky now, in a way I couldn't help him on the street that day.

He leaned forward. "You have to understand what it means to tell what you know."

"It's the truth. I'll say the same as everyone else. Bucky didn't do it."

Stick sighed. "There is no everyone else, Sam."

"There are plenty of people," I said. But I knew what he meant. I swallowed the knot that formed in my throat.

"People are afraid to testify. It's a serious thing to stand up and say the cops are lying."

"Maxie's not afraid," I said. "Did you ask her?"

Stick hesitated. "Yes. She'll do it."

"Then I'll be there too."

"Don't decide because of Maxie."

"I'm not." I paused. "The easy choice is almost never the right one, right?" Father had taught us that.

In the morning, I went back down to the hospital. I took a deep breath and stepped into Father's hospital room. He was sitting slightly propped up in bed. Mama perched in the chair beside him, leaning in. They saw me.

"Sam," they said at the same time.

"Hi." I hung by the doorway. I didn't want to do this in front of Mama, but there was no good way to ask her to leave. She must have known what I was thinking, because she stood up.

"I think I'll go find some tea." She kissed my cheek as she passed.

I moved closer to the bed. Father watched me.

"What day is it?" he asked.

"Friday."

"That's what I thought. Where should you be?"

For a second, I didn't know what he was talking about. Then I realized. "School."

Father sighed. "That makes three days in a row you've missed. I'm sure your teachers will understand, but no more, you hear?"

I nodded. "I wanted to talk to you." I took a deep breath and plunged in. "I've been asked to testify."

He frowned. "Who asked you?"

I didn't answer. He already knew. "I'm going to do it."

"I said no, and I meant it."

"Why didn't you tell me?"

"I told Steven not to get you involved in this. I told him."

"You're the one who talks about playing by the rules, about working within the system. You said I could help Bucky, but you didn't mean it, did you?"

"You don't know these people like I do," he said. "You don't know." He struggled to sit up straight, but grimaced. I moved closer to help him. He leaned back against the pillows, breathing hard. I sat on the edge of the bed.

"I think I do," I said, looking into Father's ashen face. "That's what this is about."

"You are already visible because you're my son. This will put you — don't you know I worry about you?" He took my shoulders. "Promise me, Sam, promise me you'll never pick up another gun. No matter how angry you get."

"Father — "

He looked into my eyes. "I need you to promise me, Sam. I need to hear you say you understand."

I pulled away. Father tried to hold me, but I rose to my feet, out of his reach. I could promise and he would believe me. I could say everything would be all right, and maybe it would be. But I didn't know for sure.

"Sam." The word rang like a chime in the silence, the sound rippling out over me, over everything.

"I'm sorry," I whispered.

He turned his head away. "You tell your brother that if he comes home, you can testify."

My heart skipped. "He'll come home when Bucky does," I said.

Mama and I brought Father home a few days later. Father and I sat quietly the whole way, listening to Mama chatter on about anything she could think of. As we pulled into the driveway, she finally ceased her endless monologue. The silence became huge.

I helped Father out of the car. He put his arm around my shoulder as we walked to the house. I could tell he was trying not to lean against me, but he had to, so he did.

It was a long walk to the bedroom, but we got Father situated in bed. I tried not to look in his eyes. Maybe all the things we'd left unspoken between us could remain that way.

Mama returned to the car to retrieve a few items, leaving us alone. Father seemed settled enough, so I headed for the door.

"Sam." The fragile silence shattered.

"Yes." I dropped into the chair near the bed.

"You're going through with it, then."

"Yes. We testify on Monday. I'm sorry you think it's the wrong thing."

His face took on a mix of surprise and pain. "I don't."

I sprang up. "Then how could you say no without even asking me? After I told you what I saw."

"I want you to understand."

"No one thinks I understand anything." I paced along the foot of the bed. "I get it. All of it. I do."

Father gritted his jaw and levered himself up on his

hands. "And just what understanding led you to bring a gun into this house? To take it in your hand and threaten someone's life?" His face paled a few shades and he leaned back against the pillows, releasing several quick shallow breaths.

"It wasn't even loaded."

A thin layer of fury steamrolled over Father's face, smoothing his features.

"It wasn't even loaded?" he repeated. "Do you think that even—How can you—Have you learned nothing from me?"

"I guess not," I said, knowing it would hurt him. I didn't know why I wanted to do that.

The sadness in his eyes overwhelmed me. I walked out of the room.

CHAPTER 16

STICK TOOK ME BACK TO THE PANTHER apartment to meet with Bucky's lawyers. We all sat around the table—me, Maxie, Stick, Leroy, and the two lawyers. I had met one of them before. Clive Billings was a friend of Father's, a black lawyer who had worked with the NAACP for a while. I didn't know Eric Richman, the white lawyer, who looked very natural in a tie and briefcase.

"Eric is lead counsel," Clive Billings told Maxie and me, which meant he would be the one asking us questions in court. We practiced for a while, and it was easy enough. But then they started talking about what would happen when the prosecutor questioned us.

"They may ask you about the Panthers, Sam, and we don't want to let it go there," Eric Richman said. "We'll do everything we can to prevent it. They'll have to prove that it's relevant to the case against Bucky, and we don't think they can do it."

A woman wearing the Panther leather jacket walked in, holding the hand of a girl about three years old. The little girl immediately trotted across the room to Leroy.

"There's my girl," Leroy said, scooping her up in his arms. He kissed her stomach. She giggled.

The woman laid a stack of papers on the table. "This is everything Roland suggested," she said. She lifted the child off Leroy's lap. "Come on, Nia, Daddy's working. Let's go get everybody something to eat."

"Roland?" I said, sitting up straighter. "As in, my father?" I looked at Stick. He held my gaze for a moment, then nodded.

"Roland's helping us prepare our defense," Eric Richman said. "The more heads the better on this case."

Father, who hated the Panthers? "Are you sure he's really helping?" I asked.

Stick stood so fast, the table jumped. "We've been going for a while. Can we take a break?"

Leroy nodded, stretching his arms over his head. "I, for one, could use some food," he said. "I'll go see what my wife's up to in the kitchen." He left the table.

The others began stretching as well. Stick seized my arm and practically dragged me from the table and into the next room. He shut the door behind us and released me with such force, I sat down hard on the arm of one of the chairs.

"Do you even understand what we're doing in there?" Stick demanded. His tone caught me totally off guard.

"What? Yeah, sure," I said.

"I don't think so." He paced along the bookcase in front of me, his body stiff with anger.

I rose to my feet. "What's your problem?"

Stick came forward, close to me. "This is not about me, it's about you. You say you're ready for this life, but you have no idea what it's about. And you never will until you learn to look past the surface of things."

The accusation stung. "I don't have to listen to you." I didn't need this from Stick right now. I was trying to concentrate on the trial preparations. I went for the door.

"This, right here. This is the problem with you."

"Yeah? How's that?" I tossed the words over my shoulder, halfway to the door.

"You give up too easily, Sam."

"What?" My steps faltered. "No, I don't."

"Then why am I looking at your back?"

I spun around. "I'm here to testify. I'm not walking away."

Stick shook his head. "I'm trying to talk to you, and you

don't like what you hear, so you want out. It's that way with everything. Things get a little rough, or boring, or don't go the way you want and you walk away."

"You should talk. Things are a little rough at home right now. Look who left." I lifted my chin. He *had* left first, and had left behind much more than I ever had.

"I left to *do* something. Not to get away. It's different."

"You're still gone."

His eyes flashed and I expected him to utter a crashing retort. Instead, he leaned his arms against the back of a chair and sighed. "Did you know we're going to build a clinic? Right on this block, where people can come for free?"

"I know," I lied. "I go to the classes too."

Stick sort of chuckled. A strange sound, coming from him, and not very funny. "One PE class and now you're an expert? This is a commitment, not a whim."

I could commit. I could. "I'm trying to help Bucky," I said. "What do you want from me, Stick? What?"

He pushed off the chair and stood tall. "For starters, if you have anything to say about Father, say it to me or say it to yourself. Don't bring it in here. You got that?"

"I didn't—"

"Bucky's life is on the line. Father will move any mountain he can in order to get him acquitted. Don't accuse him of being anything less than committed."

"Father doesn't want anything to do with the Panthers,"
I said. "He hates them."

Stick clamped his hand over the back of his neck and
leaned into it. "Sam, you're seeing the slim side of the
coin."

"It's true! He hates violence in all its forms, but especially
guns."

Stick sighed. "So do I, Sam," he said quietly. "How is it
that you don't know that?"

I looked up in surprise. Stick lowered himself into one
of the chairs. The anger flowed out of him, like a balloon
losing air. He rested his forearms on his thighs and ducked
his head.

"Look, as long as you think being a Panther just means
carrying a gun, you won't be able to understand what's
happening here." He kept his head down for a while and
moved his hands against each other thoughtfully.

When he finally spoke, he raised intense and weary
eyes to face me. "It's the Panthers' ideas that people fear
most, not our guns. We're telling blacks that we can fix
some of our problems ourselves, that we don't have to wait
to be accepted into the white mainstream to have our day
come."

Stick's gaze dug into mine, and he spoke with a certainty
that I wished I could feel within myself. "The guns are an

idea. Not even that, actually. They just represent an idea. It's really about a breakfast for hungry kids and the clinic that's going to go up in a year or so. I'm talking about people who have to wait for hours to get seen at a hospital, just 'cause they're black, and people who never go to a regular doctor because they cost too much."

Stick was getting crazy intense. His eyes shone. I tried to tap into his passion, but my head only filled with questions.

"It's about defending Bucky, and making sure what happened to him never happens again," Stick continued.

The mention of Bucky brought familiar images to the surface. I dealt with them, shoved them back deep into my memory. But they rose again, bringing friends this time. For once, I saw more than Bucky on the pavement. I saw his smile, his gray overalls, the orange suit he'd worn the day they brought him into the courthouse. I saw him shoveling oatmeal into his mouth, and lifting his sister Shenelle onto his shoulders.

As Stick went on, I let myself be captivated by his words, swept into his vision of the movement. I had been so deep inside Father's for so long that it felt good to rise above what I knew. I entered another space in that moment, as if I could see a corner of Stick's mind that had long been hidden from me.

"It's the difference between demonstrating and organizing," Stick said. "Between waiting for handouts that aren't coming, or taking care of each other the way we have to. It's the rock and the river, you know? They serve each other, but they're not the same thing."

Leroy knocked on the door and poked his head through. "Sandwiches," he said. "Sorry to interrupt, but it's a free-for-all in there, so I'd get a move on if I were you." He withdrew.

Stick and I sat in silence for a few more minutes. His words were still swirling in the air around us, and I breathed deeply, trying to draw them into myself.

"So now what?" I said finally.

Stick slugged my arm. "So, now we eat," he said. "Then we get you ready for court. After that, it's up to you."

CHAPTER 17

MONDAY MORNING, I WENT DOWN TO the courthouse with Maxie. We were both dressed up in our best church clothes. Maxie looked really good in the yellow dress she was wearing, with her hair pulled up in a clip. We waited in the hallway for the judge to call us inside.

Maxie slipped her hand into mine. I jumped a little.

"Other things aside," she said quietly. "I need something to hold on to."

I squeezed her hand. "This is for Bucky," I said. "We're all he's got."

"For Bucky."

I concentrated on how nice it felt to hold her hand again, and began counting the ridges on each of her knuckles. Anything to keep from thinking about why we were there. I wondered what was going through Maxie's mind.

The bailiff stuck his head through the door and called out, "Miss Maxie Brown?"

Maxie stood up and went over to him. "Here," she said. The bailiff escorted her inside. She turned her head toward me as she passed through the door. I nodded and smiled.

After what seemed like an eternity, the door reopened. Maxie emerged, the bailiff right behind her. I tried to catch Maxie's eye, but she turned away from me.

"Mr. Samuel Childs?"

I took a deep breath and went inside. The tall doors thumped shut behind me. I expected the courtroom to be huge, but it wasn't. Still, the walk to the witness stand seemed to stretch for miles. I followed the bailiff down the narrow aisle, my eyes on the nightstick dangling from his belt. I imagined everyone in the room staring at me, but I didn't look around to see for sure. The bailiff stepped aside to let me pass him into the front of the courtroom. I raised my eyes to the judge, who peered down at me through enormous eyeglasses attached to a chain around his neck.

I stepped into the witness stand, released my nervous breath and faced the court. There was Bucky, sitting between Clive Billings and Eric Richman. Several Panthers were in the audience, Stick among them. He appeared strong and confident as he nodded encouragement to me. I tried to hold my shoulders tall like him, hoping I could look strong too.

A few other people sat scattered throughout the pewlike rows, perhaps reporters, and a man with a sketchpad. He moved his pencil swiftly, glancing up at me from time to time.

Father was there, sitting with Mama across the aisle from Stick and the Panthers. He wasn't supposed to be out yet, but he wouldn't hear of me testifying without him being here. I wished his presence could make me feel better, but I worried that I wouldn't live up to what needed to be done. He would be disappointed.

I snuck a look at the jury. All men except for two women. All white. A jury of Bucky's peers. I held my breath to keep from laughing, or crying, out loud. Did they have it in them to give Bucky the benefit of the doubt? Maybe one of those men was a mechanic, at least. Maybe one of their fathers had died, and they knew what it was like to have to provide for a mother and sister when you are only eighteen.

The bailiff thrust a Bible in front of me. Over his shoulder, I met Bucky's eyes. He stared back, but his look was hollow, lacking any of his usual spark. Hopeless. I had never seen him stand so still, or go so long without a smile. It was as if the end was already given, and what I was here to do didn't matter anymore. I raised my right hand and swore to tell the truth, the whole truth and nothing but the truth.

"How did you feel?" Maxie said later. We were back at the Panther apartment, alone, except for the guards in the hall. We had returned a couple of hours ago, and collapsed onto the couch next to each other. Stick was working at the auto shop. Raheem and Leroy had stayed down at the courthouse, where the jury was deliberating. I looked at her.

"When you were up there," she said. "What did it feel like?"

"Like it wouldn't be enough," I admitted. "I'm not sure they believed me." The jury had probably made up their minds before the trial even began. It had happened a thousand times to people we knew. I didn't really know how to hope that things would work out for Bucky.

Maxie nodded. A tear slipped out of her eye and she brushed at it with her knuckles. I lifted her hand from her face. "What's wrong?"

She lowered her head. "No. It's just, what you did for Bucky—"

"What we did."

"It means more coming from you."

"Hey. Two is still better than one." I touched her chin and she smiled. "You probably said it better than me, anyway." Her smile deepened.

"We did everything we could, right?" she whispered, turning her face up to me.

I couldn't think past the tears in her eyes. I leaned in to kiss her, forgetting that I wasn't supposed to anymore. Our lips touched. I pulled back. Maxie gazed up at me.

"It's okay," she said. "I want you to." And just like that, we were back.

I leaned toward her just as Raheem burst through the door. "Not guilty!" he yelled. "The verdict is in. Not guilty! Can you believe it?"

Maxie and I jumped up. "Are you serious?" she said. I could only stare at Raheem.

"Yeow!" he whooped. He scooped Maxie up in his arms and twirled her around. "Bucky's coming home, girl!"

"Heem!" she cried. "I can't believe it!" She hugged him and he lowered her to the floor. She turned to me, a huge grin on her face. We kissed.

"Okay, break it up," Raheem said a few moments later. "That's my sister, you know."

I quickly stepped away from Maxie. I chanced a look at Raheem, expecting a glare, but he was smiling. He nodded to me ever so slightly, and I remembered that he wanted us together.

"Come on, Sam, my man." He moved toward the door. "We gotta go get Buck."

"I'm coming too," Maxie said.

Raheem pointed to the desk. "Someone has to stay and make the calls."

Maxie shot him a look. "And I guess that's the girl's job."

"You got it, little sister," Raheem said, chucking her under the chin. Maxie looked to me. I shrugged. It wasn't my call. I hardly got to go anywhere either, so I wasn't going to mess up my chance by crossing Raheem.

Maxie narrowed her eyes at me as she scooped up the calling lists. I might be worse off for crossing her.

"Maybe she could come," I said. "I'll help make calls later."

"Don't start," Raheem warned. "I don't want you to come either, but Bucky asked for you." He walked out.

"Don't say I didn't try," I said to Maxie as I trailed him out the door. She made a face.

Downstairs, Raheem was unlocking Leroy's car. He pulled four shotguns from the backseat and held two out to me. "Trunk."

I hesitated, and Raheem raised his eyebrows. My

fingers closed around the neck of each gun. I thought of Father. Did I do the right thing by not promising him, by leaving him to worry about me every minute? I frowned.

Raheem shrugged. "It's Bucky's day. No guns."

"Okay." I placed the guns carefully on the floor of the trunk. Bucky wouldn't want them up front.

We went by Roy Dack's to tell Stick the news. Stick and Roy both came bursting out of the garage as Raheem pulled in, honking madly.

Raheem and I exchanged a glance. "Not guilty!" we yelled out the windows. Stick nearly fell over. We jumped out of the car and went over to him.

"I can't believe it." Stick clasped hands with Raheem, then turned to me.

"You did it," he said, hugging me tight. "You did it." His praise filled me up. I didn't know what to say.

"We're going to get him now," Raheem said. "Can you come?" We all looked at Roy.

The older man sniffed. "Four hours to go on your shift, and you're asking to take off."

"No, sir," Stick said quickly. "Not at all."

The wrinkles in Roy's cheeks shifted as he rolled his mouth a few times. "I suppose it won't hurt me to lose one evening's help," he said. He patted Stick's arm. "Go get our boy. Bring him home."

"Thanks, Roy." Stick grinned. "I'll make up the time."

Roy waved his hand. "No, no. Go on now."

We returned to the car. Stick maneuvered out of the coveralls as we drove. "They're all yours again, Buck," he murmured, tossing them in the backseat. "Where's my coat?"

"In the back," Raheem said. I handed Stick his jacket and beret.

We picked up Bucky at the courthouse. He jumped in the backseat with me and tapped the back of the passenger seat, where Stick was seated. "Get me outta here," he said, smiling.

"You got it, brother," Raheem said, then whooped loudly, honking the horn as he pulled into traffic. The rest of us followed suit, cheering, stomping feet and pounding doors.

"All right, all right," Stick said, waving a hand. "Leroy probably wants his car back in one piece."

We stopped the frantic celebrating, but everyone was jubilant. Even though we wouldn't have admitted it out loud, in our wildest dreams, we never thought Bucky would be acquitted.

"I think he'll be happier to have Bucky back in one piece," I said, nudging him with my fist.

Bucky caught my neck in the crook of his elbow and

knuckled my hair. I couldn't believe how skinny his arm felt against me. "Hey, I knew you missed me," he said. Then his tone turned serious. "Thanks. For standing up for me. You don't know —"

"Hey," I said, brushing off his thanks even though the words reached deep inside me. "Of course." I met Stick's eyes in the rearview mirror. A crazy, awkward gladness filled me. Maybe, finally, I had done something right.

Raheem launched into a funny story. From time to time I caught Stick studying me in the mirror, and we would laugh together in a way we never had before. When I wasn't concentrating on Stick, I watched Bucky. The spring was back in his movements, and his eyes twinkled as he grinned his toothy grin. There was an edge to his laugh, though, a hardness that I figured was leftover fear. He would be back to normal again before long. Bucky always bounced back; that was his life.

We laughed harder than I could remember doing in a while. Everything had seemed so heavy, so serious for such a long time. Something great was happening here. Between me and Stick, between me and Bucky, between all of us. I could barely believe that I'd had a part in making it possible.

We had almost made it back into the neighborhood,

when lights flashed and a siren blipped behind us.

"I always knew you had a lead foot, Raheem," Bucky said. He half smiled as if he was still joking with us, but no one laughed.

I caught Raheem's worried glance in the rearview mirror, and my stomach tightened.

"Look at the speedometer," Raheem said to Stick under his breath.

"I see it. Just pull over. It's worse if you don't."

Raheem eased the car onto the shoulder of the road. I peered out the back window. Both officers emerged from the squad car and approached us, pistols drawn. One came up to Raheem's window.

"Is there a problem, Officers? I believe I was driving below the speed limit."

"License and registration. Move slowly."

Raheem removed his license from his wallet and handed it to the officer. "And registration?" the officer said, nodding.

Stick lifted his hand to the glove compartment. He flipped the latch and the little door fell open.

The gun! It was still sitting there, where Leroy had shoved it when we'd raced away from the demonstration. I had forgotten all about it, and from the way he jerked his hand back, I could tell Stick had too.

"Gun!" the cop at the window shouted. He fired two rounds. The explosion of sound started me shaking. Bucky clawed his fingers into the seat between us, letting out air in a desperate sigh.

"All of you, out of the car," the cop screamed. "Now!" The shots still echoed in my ears.

My heart thumped as I opened the door. Raheem got out of the driver's seat and Bucky did the same. I was halfway out of the car when I noticed Stick hadn't moved. I looked over. His hand fell away from his chest, a pool of red in his palm.

The cop was shouting at me to get out of the car, to keep my hands where he could see them. My fingers curled around the top of the half-lowered window.

"Stick?" I said.

He turned his head toward me. The look in his eyes said everything. Then Raheem's hands were on me, pulling me away from the car.

I fought it. "No!"

"On your knees!" the cop said. "Hands in the air."

"Stick!" I screamed, straining against Raheem's grip.

"They'll shoot you." Raheem spoke into my ear. "Do you hear me? If you go near him, they will shoot you."

"On the ground!" The cop waved his gun at us.

Raheem squeezed me tighter. "Do it," he said as he

released me. He dropped to his knees beside me. Bucky was already down.

A trembling calm came over me as Raheem moved away. I stopped screaming and stood still. The cop motioned me to the ground with a jerk of his head. Behind him stood his partner, gun still pointing toward the open car window.

I didn't look at the car, at Stick. Instead, I looked at the cop as I kneeled in front of him. The naked hatred in his eyes struck me deep. He was ready to kill me.

"Sam." Stick's soft call tore through me. Through the open backseat door, I could see into the car. Stick was sitting in his seat, his head turned toward me. I had to get to him. I lifted one knee off the ground and put my foot down.

"Sam, no," Stick whispered.

"On your knees," the cop shouted. I had to get to Stick, but I couldn't.

"It's my brother," I shouted. "Please."

"On your knees, or I'll shoot!"

I dropped my leg, never tearing my eyes from Stick. He was just a few yards away. I could see the blood running out of him, spilling over his hands and onto the car seat. He leaned against the headrest and closed his eyes.

"Stick!"

His eyes opened, zooming in on me.

"I'm sorry," I told him, mouthing the words. I felt sick inside, but Stick seemed calm, so calm, it was strange.

"It's okay. It's going to be okay," he murmured, closing his eyes.

"Stick!" I shouted again. He didn't open his eyes.

Everything became still.

The air.

My body.

The entire world around me. The horror transpiring in front of me, suspended for one disbelieving instant.

Until then, I had never known anger, the kind of coiling rage that slid sharp through my gut. I had never known how much one moment could hurt.

"Face down on the ground," the cop yelled. But I was stuck, my eyes locked on Stick. The cop stepped closer, cutting off my view.

In my mind I was leaping forward, lunging at the cop. My fingers clawed out his throat, our hands grappling together for control, our bodies straining to learn who would live and who would die. The urge was so alive within me that I had no idea what force was keeping me still.

The cop grabbed the back of my head and shoved my face into the pavement. That was real. Tiny pebbles scratched my cheeks and nose, and I choked on the smell of tar and rubber. The handcuffs squeezed cold and tight against my wrists. I pinched my eyes shut, tried to close my ears to the sound of sirens and the voices of cops. A stream of "what ifs" flooded my mind. But it was too late to change anything.

CHAPTER 18

RAHEEM AND I SAT QUIETLY IN THE SMALL cell, waiting for word of Stick. It seemed we had been locked up for hours, but they wouldn't tell us anything.

"He's going to be all right," I said. Stick always made everything all right.

Raheem said nothing. I jumped up and paced the length of the cell. My shoulder ached where one of the cops had kicked me, but it was nothing compared to the knot of fear in my stomach.

"Where did they take Bucky?"

"It's worse for him, because he just got out."

"But he's not guilty," I said. "They decided." I spoke the words, but they were meaningless. It didn't matter what happened in court. I should have known.

Raheem fingered the bruise along his jaw, which had begun to swell. "They weren't going to let him go," he said.

"It doesn't work like that. We just didn't think it would happen so soon."

The truth settled into my bones. If they wanted Bucky, they could have him. They could do anything they wanted.

Why had I even testified? What was the point? I cringed inside at the thought. Stick was right about me. Here it was, after the fact, and I was still trying to walk away. I shook off the doubt. I had testified, and Bucky was set free. For a short while, he'd been free.

"How can they be mad at Bucky? They lied. He didn't do anything."

"Tell a story a certain way enough times, and you start to believe it," Raheem said. "Doesn't matter if you know it isn't true."

I walked to the door of the cell and looked down the hall. No sign of anyone. I gripped the bars. "Stick's going to be all right," I whispered.

A door slammed. Muffled voices echoed along the hall.

"Sam," Raheem said suddenly. "Don't answer any questions. You know that, right?"

"Yeah, okay," I said. Heavy footsteps approached.

"Look at me." Raheem spun me around and held my shoulders. "Don't tell them anything until your dad is sitting next to you. You hear me? Anything."

"All right," I said. The look in his eyes was scaring me.

Three cops appeared. They led us out of the cell and upstairs. They put Raheem into one room and me into another. I sat in the only chair at the table, facing the big mirror. My reflection startled me. The side of my face was scratched from the pavement and my hair puffed unevenly. I almost closed my eyes, but I didn't. Was someone watching me through the glass?

A cop in uniform and a man in a suit came in. They closed the door and stood across the table from me. I had to lean my head back to look at their faces.

"How're you doing, there, boy?" the man in the suit said. His eyes narrowed a bit when I didn't answer.

"Let's talk about how you got here," the cop said. He moved to the wall and leaned against it. His hand rested against the nightstick at his belt. "Why don't you tell us what happened?"

"I want to see my father," I said. "Can I call him?"

They glanced at each other. "He's on his way," the man in the suit said. "We just have a few questions for you while we're waiting." He sat on the edge of the table nearest me. I pushed my chair back.

He chuckled. "It's all right, Sam. We're all friends here."

I folded my hands, squeezing them together hard. The

man's eyes glinted as he watched my movement. "A few simple questions, Sam, nothing serious. Let's start with who was in the car with you."

I stared at my hands.

"Now, son, you know we already know who you were with." The soothing tone of his voice made me feel sick. He reached into his jacket and withdrew a pair of glasses. I saw his badge hanging from his vest pocket. I'd seen that kind of badge before, on the Special Agents who came to observe Father's demonstrations.

"Raheem Brown was driving, wasn't he? Yes, that's what it says here." The agent flipped through the file in his hand. "And Clarence Willis?"

"And then there's the young man in the front passenger seat. Your brother, I believe?" He peered at me over his glasses. "He took two bullets to the chest. You'd like to know how he's doing, wouldn't you?"

I trembled in my seat. It was all I could do not to nod, not to beg him to tell me Stick was all right.

"I'll tell you." He studied his fingernails, then locked eyes with me. "As soon as you tell me what you know about the Black Panther Party."

I closed my eyes. The table creaked as the agent stood up. I felt him pass behind me.

"No, let's come back to that later," he said. "I'm still

therockandtheriver

interested in what happened at the car." He moved around the room like a shark, circling me.

"And then there are the rifles to think about. Four, I believe. All loaded." He consulted the file. "In the backseat, weren't they? Right at your feet?"

I jerked. The agent slowly removed his glasses and tucked them into his breast pocket. "Something you wanted to say, Sam?"

I blew out my breath. If Stick were here, he wouldn't play this game. I clung to that thought. I tried to close my ears, to look away from the agent's slick grin.

"As I was saying, the officers are taking prints off the guns now."

My eyes widened. I knew I shouldn't react, but I couldn't help it. The agent chuckled.

"Don't be afraid, Sam. I'm not going to let anything happen to you. In fact, I'm willing to forget all about this, if you can provide me with a little information."

My heart thumped. I tried to swallow, but my mouth went dry.

"You, Raheem, Clarence," he paused. "Your brother. We'll let everybody go."

He leaned closer to me, lowering his voice. "Are you a member of the Black Panthers?"

I could barely breathe. I knew I shouldn't speak, but

maybe if I said no, he would leave me alone.

The door opened. The agent turned to face the cop who entered. "What is it?" he snapped. The cop jerked his head, motioning the agent into the hall. Father's voice boomed outside, demanding to see me. I relaxed a bit, knowing he had come for me.

They brought Raheem and me out a while later, and told us we could go. Father was standing near the front desk. I stopped. I didn't want to go over to him.

"No," I said backing toward Raheem. "I don't want him to take me. I want Stick."

"Go with your dad, Sam," Raheem said. "Go home."

"Where is Stick?" I said. "Where is he?" But I already knew. I knew the moment I saw Father's face.

Father crossed the room.

"No," I said, trying to step behind Raheem, who moved out of the way.

"Sam." Father placed his arm around my shoulders. "He's gone. He died a few hours ago."

I should have felt something. Anything. But I didn't. I walked toward the door. Father followed me out to the parking lot.

"I'm not going with you," I said. I hadn't planned to say it, it just came out. I kept walking.

"Sam, you are going to get in that car, and we are going home."

I ignored him.

"I thought I raised you boys to make good decisions," Father said, breathing hard as he tried to keep up with my pace. He should have been home, in bed, but he had come for me. Still, I didn't slow down. "You're taking after Steven now," he said.

My stomach churned. I welcomed the feeling, let it fill the void in me. I turned to face Father. "Don't blame him. He didn't do anything wrong."

"I want to know what you were doing in that car."

The anger returned then, in a way I hadn't imagined possible. Anger can come into you so tangibly, so physically it's like a separate person. As if someone enters your body, stands there with one fist in your throat and the other tight around your gut. It's like tears you can't cry, but stronger, more insistent. Deeper. And it won't let go. It's cramped and it's crying, but it won't let go.

"Stick is dead!" I shouted. "None of the other things matter."

"Don't raise your voice to me."

"Don't tell me what to do."

His eyes smoldered. "I haven't even begun."

Out of nowhere, his arms hooked around me, locking

me to his chest. "Sam. Sam," he whispered into my hair. I could feel his heart beating, sense the sorrow in his frame.

I shoved away and ran. Father called after me, his voice breaking on my name. He couldn't come after me.

I ran until Father's voice faded behind me, until sweat poured into my eyes and onto my cheeks, until I choked on the air whipping against my face. I tumbled to my knees in a patch of grass, letting my forehead and my fingers touch the earth.

"Stick," I whispered. I spoke his name over and over into the dirt, until my voice faded into nothing.

CHAPTER 19

THE LAKE WAS A SHORT DISTANCE AWAY. I had no idea I had run so far. I took off my shoes and walked down to the water. Each wave lapped at my toes with a sound like a whisper. I stood surrounded by water and sky, and it seemed the night could swallow me.

I remained still and silent, but the creature within me growled its way deeper and deeper into my soul. I lost my sense of time, just standing in the dark. Reliving the events that had led me to this place. The red wetness in Stick's palm. The sound of my own screams. The hate in the cop's eyes, the reciprocal hate blossoming within myself. The clang of holding cell bars. The interrogation room mirror and its thousand invisible eyes. The agent's oily grin, trying to grease me for information I didn't even have. And somewhere, hiding at the back of it all, the ache that, moments before, I'd been so happy over Bucky's release. We'd all been laughing.

Stick, gone.

The unfairness of it overwhelmed me. Bucky hadn't deserved to go to trial for a meaningless accident. Raheem had not been speeding. Father, stabbed, who had never lifted a finger to hurt anyone. None of them deserved what had happened. Least of all, Stick, who had done nothing but leave a gun in a tower. It should have been me. I deserved it, I deserved it all.

The water rushed in and out around me. A second pair of bare feet appeared beside mine in the sand. Maxie was standing next to me. How had she found me? When had she come? Her warm fingers slipped into mine. She pressed my hand.

I blinked, suddenly alert. Maxie whispered, "I'm so sorry," but the lake swallowed the sound of her voice. Silent tears rushed down her face as we stood there, our wet toes touching. We stood there for a long time, while the night settled in more deeply. The wind off the water grew cool.

Maxie held my hand as we walked back up to the grass. We sat on a bench and put our shoes on. Maxie cried into my shoulder, hugging me tight. My own tears had gone.

"I'll walk home with you," she said.

I lowered my head. "I can't go home yet." I couldn't get

a grip on what was happening, but it was all my fault.

"Come home with me, then."

I had nowhere else to go. We headed for her block.

Maxie opened the door to her apartment and pushed me through ahead of her. Raheem was pacing beside the window. He stopped when we walked in. Father was sitting on the sofa.

"Thank you, Maxie," Father said, standing up.

I stepped back. "You knew he was here?" I asked Maxie.

"He was worried about you." She moved closer, placing her hand on my arm. I yanked it away.

"I can't believe this. I told you I wasn't—and you—"

"You should be with your family," Maxie whispered. The clock on the wall ticked its way closer to one A.M. Maxie's betrayal stung. I turned to leave.

I'd never seen Father move so fast. He got between me and the door before I even had my hand out to turn the knob.

"You are coming home with me, Sam. It is not open to discussion." His voice held its familiar thunder, but he pressed his hand against the side of his body, wincing as he spoke.

No one moved. Father couldn't make me go with him,

keklamagoon

and he knew it. But I couldn't stand the pained look in his eyes.

"You're supposed to be resting," I said. It sounded stupid to my own ears.

Father stepped forward. He put his arms around me, and the part of me that wanted to run away again shut down. He held me so tight, I forgot what had happened and for a moment, everything was okay. Then he let go.

"Your mother needs to see you," he said. "To know you're all right."

Raheem crossed the room. "Sam." He folded me in an awkward hug. I was too surprised to return it. He spoke in my ear. "I'm going to find the cop who did this. You can count on that."

I pulled back. The cold light in Raheem's eyes matched the tone of his whispered promise: this wasn't over yet. I nodded.

Maxie slipped between Raheem and me. She hugged me in her gentle, knowing way, but it didn't make me feel close to her.

All the lights were on, and there were several cars in the driveway when we drove up. Father parked at the curb. We sat in the car without speaking for a moment, then I got out. Father followed. He pulled a bag from the backseat and carried it inside with us. A black leather sleeve poked out of the bag. Stick's clothes. My stomach tightened.

At the door, Father paused, his hand on the knob. "Thank you," he said. "We love you very much, you know."

I nodded, looking away.

Mama was sitting on the sofa, twisting a handkerchief in her hands. Leon Betterly's wife and two ladies from the church sat with her. She jumped up and came to me. She ran her hands over my arms and smoothed back my hair. She whispered against my cheeks as she kissed me.

Mama clutched my shirt and looked over my shoulder at Father. She cried out, moving around me, and tore the bag from Father's hand. Stick's clothes spilled onto the floor. Jacket, shoes, socks, belt, beret. His shirt and pants were missing. I shook my head to erase the image of Stick's blood rushing over them.

Mama hugged the leather jacket to her. She dropped to the floor, rocking back and forth on her knees. The other women put their hands on her. Their quiet cries made my ears ache.

I went to my bedroom and closed the door, but I could still hear them. I lay down and pressed the pillow over my ears. It blocked the sounds from the other room, but it couldn't block the pain. I didn't want to feel, or think, but

I was overrun. Stick was everywhere, in my head, in my heart.

The door opened.

"Don't go away from me," Mama whispered, touching my cheeks. Her tears dripped on the backs of my hands. She sat beside me until I fell asleep.

I woke in the middle of the night to the sound of tapping at the window. I leaped out of bed and stumbled across the room. I pushed the curtains aside.

"Stick?" I said, yanking open the window. Cool air brushed my face. Night sounds surrounded me, but no one was there. I sat on the edge of Stick's bed, holding the curtain in my fist, staring out into the night.

In the morning, Father knocked on the door. When I didn't answer, he came in, anyway. His eyes misted when he saw me curled up on Stick's bed by the window. He cleared his throat.

"I'd like to talk about what happened yesterday," he said. I closed my eyes.

The mattress shifted as he sat down beside me. "It's a terrible time, Sam, but I need you to tell me about it."

I lay still. I couldn't tell him anything. I couldn't stand to think about what had happened, though it played over and over in my mind. After a few minutes, Father left me alone.

I sat up. Stick's leather jacket lay on the foot of his bed, where Mama must have left it the night before. I touched the cool, smooth leather. My fingers moved over the rough-edged hole in the front. I shivered.

At the foot of my bed, the block tower loomed, jagged and leering. The mess of blocks still all over the floor, because I hadn't had the energy to deal with it since then. The sight of it made me queasy—this thing Stick and I had built together, and half destroyed together. And now he was gone. It meant nothing without him. I leaped across the room, throwing my body into the tower, thrashing my arms and legs until it was nothing but a cascade of blocks upon the floor.

In the brief moments it took to tear down our years of work, I felt nothing. I had no thoughts, not one glimmer of intention. I was fueled purely by the desperate need to make something happen. But the tower caved into rubble long before the feeling was satisfied.

Breathing hard, I stood among the spilled blocks, surveying the damage I'd done. It wasn't enough. I thought back to Raheem's whispered vow, to find the cop who'd taken Stick from me, from the world. I breathed easier then. There was one other thing I could make happen.

One other thing that might balance what had happened.

I took a roll of dark tape from the hall closet and patched the hole in Stick's jacket with a wide X. Then I slipped it on. The shoulders drooped onto my arms a bit, and the sleeves hung past my wrists, but it felt nice.

CHAPTER 20

THE SUN STUNG MY EYES AS I STARED OUT the car window at the cemetery lawn. The car had stopped, but we sat waiting for Mama to compose herself a little so we could walk to the graveside.

As Mama wept against him, Father looked across the car at me. He was surely thinking about how I'd disappointed him, how I'd ruined everything for all of us. I wasn't as good as he thought I was. The stunned look on his face when I'd come out of my room this morning wearing Stick's jacket had said it all.

I got out of the car. Maxie was standing with Raheem and Bucky at the edge of the crowd. They turned as I walked up.

I looked straight at Raheem. No words necessary.

He nodded once. "Name. Address."

The fist in my gut knotted tighter. He'd found the cop.

Maxie touched my sleeve. "Steve's jacket?" she whispered. I turned away from her without answering. She'd come by the house, they told me, but I didn't come out of my room to see her. I hadn't come out to see anybody, actually, but especially not Maxie.

"It's too big for you," Raheem said, straightening the jacket shoulders.

"He'll grow into it." I turned to see Leroy standing behind me. He pulled me aside. "Are you sure you want to do this?" he said quietly. "Have you thought about it?" His tone said he knew what Raheem was planning.

"I have to," I said.

Leroy shifted his gaze to Raheem. "A word, please." They walked away from us. I steadily ignored Maxie, facing Bucky instead. Maxie touched my arm again, then left us alone.

Bucky shook my hand. "I'm real sorry, Sam," he said. "I wish—" He shrugged and stared at the ground. "I guess you know."

I moved closer to him. "Later, I'm going with Raheem to get the cop. You could come."

Bucky's eyes widened. "That's not my scene," he said. He paused. "It wasn't Steve's either, Sam."

Yes, it was. It was. "After everything, you don't care about fighting back?"

"You know that's not it."

"He gave up his life fighting for you, and you won't do anything to repay that?"

"That's between me and Steve."

I made myself as tall as I could. "Well, he's not here, so now it's between you and me."

Bucky shook his head. I followed his gaze over my shoulder to the group of Panthers heading toward us from the front gate. "I go to work every day, Sam. I bring home some cash so my family can eat, so we can live. I'm not stuck up in jail because of what they did. I had a job to come back to." Tears shone in his eyes, and he brushed a few off his cheeks. "You think I'm not grateful? Look again."

Bucky pulled back his shoulders. "I'm sorry that he's gone. I can't bring him back. But I'm not going to blow this." He turned and walked away, joining the other mourners at the graveside. I let him go. I didn't need his help, or anyone's.

I went toward Leroy and Raheem. They were speaking in low tones, but gesturing loudly at each other. They didn't notice me.

"This is not what we're about," Leroy said as I approached.

"I'm not talking about 'us.' I'm talking about me. And Sam. We're doing it."

"Don't twist Sam up in your mess. He's got enough to deal with. Anyway, the cops won't see the distinction between you and us. You're opening us up for real trouble. Don't go out looking for a fight."

"We're already in real trouble," Raheem said. "They come after us, we go after them. How many times have you said it? It's time for the world to know that we're not gonna cower in fear when they put a gun to our heads, because we've got one pointing back at them!"

"Yes, and you'll hear me say it again. They're getting the message. But not like this."

"Stop," I said. They turned to me. "It's decided."

Father and Mama had gotten out of the car and were coming over. Raheem and Leroy joined Maxie and the others at the far side of the grave. A lot of the Panthers had come out for the funeral. My eyes roamed the sea of black leather.

Father and Mama put their arms around each other as Reverend Downe began his eulogy for Stick. I stood a little apart from them. The Reverend's words were no doubt thoughtful, but I couldn't stand to listen to them.

I gazed across the open grave at Maxie. She stared

back. I couldn't remember what she had done that I was supposed to be mad at her for. It suddenly didn't matter. I moved through the crowd around the edge of the grave until I reached her. The other Panthers stood nearby. Several of them touched my shoulder as I passed. At the other side, Father turned his face into the side of Mama's head and closed his eyes.

When Reverend Downe finished speaking, Leroy stepped forward. "Mr. Childs asked me to say a few words," he said. I looked at Father. He was watching Leroy.

Leroy spoke for a while, but I couldn't concentrate on his words. People cried as he shared his thoughts, but my mind raced far from the graveside. There was a heaviness in my chest and stomach that I couldn't breathe out or digest.

Maxie pulled away from me, taking a tissue from her skirt pocket. I hadn't realized I was leaning on her until she moved. Suddenly, it was hard to stand.

A strong arm wrapped around my neck from behind. Raheem pulled me back against him. I was grateful not to have fallen. He breathed against my ear. "Steady, there. You okay?"

"Yes."

Raheem tucked something along my spine into the

waist of my pants. I didn't have to reach for it to know what it was. Raheem patted my shoulder then withdrew his arm, his jaw set at a decisive angle. I moved my own jaw side to side until it relaxed.

I stared at the coffin and the square pit of earth. I brought my arms close against my chest as another chill coursed through me. Stick. I didn't want to think of him in a box. In a hole.

Mindless of the crowds, the service going on, I knelt beside the coffin, putting my hands on the smooth wood. I lowered my head and stared at my knees. My black suit pants stood out against the white tarp stretched beneath the coffin. I pinched my eyes shut.

When I lifted my head, Father was looking down at me from the other side of the coffin. He stood so still, so quiet, so sure that one might mistake him for a statue if not for the tears rushing unheeded over his face. For just the second time, in all my life, I watched my father cry. I hated with every ounce of my being the force that had caused him such pain. Even more, I despised my part in bringing it.

But now, I could put everything right.

I rose to my feet, and a calm swept over me. I caught my breath to keep from crying out loud. Stick was with me. I felt his whisper in the echo of my heartbeat. *Sam. It's all up to you now.*

I nodded, drying my eyes on the sleeve of Stick's jacket. My jacket. I couldn't let him down. I knew what I had to do.

I touched the side of the coffin one last time and returned to stand by Raheem. "Let's go," I said. "Right now."

CHAPTER 21

THINGS INSIDE ME BEGAN TO MOVE VERY fast. Raheem and I emerged from the cemetery and headed for Leroy's car.

I rounded the car to the passenger seat. Along the grassy slope of the cemetery I saw my father approaching. And of all the things I felt capable of in that moment, facing him was not one.

"Let's go," I said to Raheem. In the side mirror I watched Leroy meet Father in the street. He put his hand on Father's arm and led him back toward the funeral.

Raheem drove intently, hands tight upon the steering wheel. I didn't ask where we were going, where the cop lived. I didn't want to know his name. Even holding the gun, I didn't feel tough.

My fingers tightened around Stick's gun. It was more mine than his, anyway. He hadn't meant to, but he'd given it to me.

Raheem slammed on the brakes for a red light. The gun slid off my lap onto the floor. By reflex, I braced my hand against the glove compartment. That's when it hit me.

I was sitting where Stick had sat when he died. With no more warning than that, I felt him there. With me, inside me. A sensation so strong that I nearly screamed aloud.

You said I couldn't follow through on anything, Stick. You'll see. You said I ought to make up my mind, then do what I set out to do.

This isn't what I meant.

No? Well, this is what you get, Stick. This is what you get for leaving me.

Here again, that gut-gnawing sensation. Full to brimming with rage and no outlet. None except the one at my feet. I bent forward and retrieved the gun.

The motion triggered a sharp memory, one that was never far from me anymore. Stick, shot and bleeding. Stick, looking to me for help—something he never, ever did. When he'd needed me most, I couldn't be there. I drowned in recollection of the cop's hateful look, the way he'd shoved my face into the ground. The fact that the handcuffs and his boot on my shoulder had kept me from reaching Stick in his last living moments.

The thought twisted my core into hopeless knots, tight enough to carry me to a place where I could see only action, no consequences. Where I could feel myself pull the trigger and things could still turn out okay. I saw myself, gun in hand, standing tall over the cop. Killing his power.

The deep intention separated me from every other thing in existence. Me and my rage, alone. Nothing to weigh me down, to make me think, to make me ache. I hit some other plane, a space of no pain, no future, no consequence, no next moment, no regret, only this: a gun and a score to settle. I felt free.

Then the air around me broke. It had lasted long, so long, that the return of conscience shook me. I actually trembled in my seat. I had touched a place previously unimaginable to me.

"Stop the car," I said. Raheem looked over at me. We were still at the red light. I opened the door and got out, closing it behind me. I lodged the gun under my belt and leaned against the car, trying to clear my head.

Raheem's door popped too. "What?"

"We have to stop," I said. But the feeling lingered, loose inside me. The promise of something able to free me from this guilt. Revenge.

I turned away from the car, battling the urge to get back in and keep going. I scanned the street, not certain what I was even looking for. Then I realized where we were.

The light was green. Several cars honked at us, but

therockandtheriver

273

Raheem waved them around. He stood in the V of the open car door, watching as I went up on the sidewalk.

"This is it," I called to him. "The clinic Stick was telling me about." It was a wide, two-story building, one lot away from the corner. The windows were covered in newspaper and the door with a smattering of work permits and construction bills. Stretched across three upstairs windows was a huge red and black banner stamped with the Party's panther logo, proclaiming:

Neighborhood <u>Free</u> Health Clinic
Opening Soon!

"Yeah. So what?" Raheem said.

I studied the building for a long moment. Would it become everything Stick had wanted it to be? If it did, I wanted to be there to see. More than that, I wanted to make sure it happened.

"So what?" Raheem repeated. "Let's go already."

I came back to the car. Raheem seemed to know I'd changed my mind before I even opened my mouth. He pounded the roof as I got closer. "Steve was my friend. That cop is going to pay."

"He was my brother." I felt the tears coming back. I pulled the gun from my waistband and stared at it. "What does it mean if we go after the cop? If we—kill him."

"He deserves it."

"Because he killed Stick. Because he's a cop. Because he's white."

"Yes." Raheem practically trembled with readiness. I recognized it because the same tremor still ran within me.

I fingered the cool metal. Raheem stood silent, waiting.

"I can't do it." I slid the gun across the car roof. Raheem caught it with one hand. "Stick wouldn't want me to."

"Come on, man, don't be soft."

"I'm not doing it." I opened the car door, but it wasn't that easy. The gun in Raheem's hand now pointed at me.

"Steve would want justice," he shouted. "We can give him that!"

"He wanted the clinic opened," I countered. "He wanted safe streets, and a bigger breakfast program. We can give him that."

The gun remained steady in Raheem's hand, but his voice wavered. "It's not enough."

It wasn't. Nothing ever would be.

I stared over the barrel at Raheem. "You gonna shoot me, or what?"

Raheem blinked. He stuck the gun in his jacket and got behind the wheel. He leaned his head forward, resting it on the backs of his hands. I sat, leaning against the headrest, eyes closed. Me, in Stick's place. Now and forever.

"Take me back, please. I'm missing my brother's funeral."

Raheem didn't speak to me at all on the ride back. I didn't care. He pulled onto the street by the cemetery, parking among a long row of cars, then strode off down the street, a determined look in his eyes. I called after him, but he didn't look back.

The service had ended. People were leaving, trailing in small clusters toward parked cars and bus stops. I walked up onto the grass, staying rather apart from the crowds. A few departing people came up and shook my hand or hugged me, but I didn't really pay attention to them. Father walked Mama to the car, his arm around her shoulders. He helped her get seated, then turned and headed back toward me. He crossed the grass slowly, weaving among the headstones, his eyes fixed on me as he approached.

The weight inside me was no lighter for my recent change of heart. My chest felt closed. No relief yet for the knots lurking within. Father and I stood without speaking for a while. Baby birds chirped from within the budding trees like nothing was out of the ordinary. Their sweet voices pricked my ears, and the sun that warmed them stung my eyes until they began to overflow.

"Go on with Mama. I'll be home later," I said. "I want to stay here a while." I brushed my wrist over my eyes so he wouldn't see me crying. But Father wasn't so easily fooled.

"I'll wait," he said. "I'm not leaving you here alone."

"I'll drive him home, Roland," Leroy said, walking over to us. He placed one arm around my shoulder, and extended the other to Father, who shook it. They exchanged a long glance. Finally, Father nodded.

"All right then. I'll see you soon, Sam." He held my arm for a moment, then walked away. I glanced up at Leroy with new respect. He'd gotten Father to change his mind. No argument, no discussion. I'd rarely seen that happen.

"You want to talk?" Leroy said, the words so gentle, I wanted to lean into them.

I squared my shoulders. "I didn't do what you think."

"I hope," Leroy said, "you did exactly what I think. And that there are still six bullets in that gun."

For the second time in as many minutes, I looked at him anew. "There were when I left it," I said. "But Raheem was pretty upset."

Leroy nodded sagely. "He'll be okay."

"How did you know I wouldn't do it?"

"There's a lot of your brother in you."

At that, I had to walk away. I turned up the hill,

approaching Stick's coffin, now sitting alone on the grass. Leroy would wait.

I lingered for a while at the graveside, trying to burn this spot into my mind as Stick's new place in the world. It was hard, but for once in my life, I didn't want to walk away.

I could have said the things that had never been said between us before—I love you, I understand now—but words didn't matter anymore. Somehow, I knew Stick could feel what I felt.

The cemetery workers began rolling up the tarp, preparing to put the coffin in the ground. I couldn't stand to watch that part, and anyway, it was time to go home. I let my heart say the last good-bye because I couldn't manage it with my breath.

Leroy was waiting patiently at his car. He nodded when he saw me coming. "Ready to go?"

"Raheem's gonna do it, isn't he?"

"I don't think so. He'll cool off." Leroy tapped my arm. "Come on. I'll drive you home." He climbed into the driver's seat. I hesitated before opening the passenger door.

"I wanted to do it," I said, getting in. "I still do."

"I hear you."

Leroy drove in silence for a while, resting his elbow on the door and gripping the wheel lightly with his fingertips.

"Your father would be proud of you, though."

I shook my head. "I'm not sure he would be."

"He is, Sam. Says it all the time."

"Not lately." I looked over as I registered what he had said. Father and Leroy? "He told you that? When?"

Leroy's mouth curved gently, as if he knew a secret that he wasn't going to tell. "I'm not sure. I talk to him a lot."

"About what?"

Leroy shrugged. "Anything. My ideas. His ideas. The movement."

"He listens to you talk about the Panthers?"

"Yeah." Leroy looked at me out the corner of his eye.

"Then you know he doesn't get it."

"He's a smart man, Sam. He gets it. He just doesn't agree with our methods."

"*I* can't talk to him about it."

"It's different," Leroy said. "I'm not his son. Though, I've known your father since I was your age, about. He's a great leader. This whole community looks up to him. I got involved in the movement because of him. The first time I heard him speak—" He shook his head. "I'm telling you, Sam. This fire started inside me, and I thought, *There really is something I can do.* It's a gift, to be able to make people feel that."

I thought about how many times I'd seen Father shake

entire crowds with his words. I remembered too, Leroy's passionate speech at the first political education class I'd attended.

"I think you have it too," I said.

Leroy looked pleased, but thoughtful. "Maybe. I hope so."

The car slowed for a traffic light.

"Turn left," I said when the light changed. Leroy maneuvered the car onto the adjacent street as if it had been his plan to turn all along, but it hadn't. He didn't comment as he pulled up in front of the Panthers' apartment building. We walked inside together.

Maxie was sitting with Lester on the couch. She jumped up when she saw me. I started toward her.

"Hold on. We're not finished." Leroy held my sleeve and led me toward the back room. He closed the door behind us, then eased into one of the armchairs. "What changed your mind?"

I walked to the window. My fingers traced the edge of the sill, chasing shadows. Would I ever look out a window and not think of Stick?

I moved along the bookcase, toward the center of the room, so I was facing Leroy. "It's hard to explain," I told him.

"What are you going to tell your father?" Leroy had

a knack for getting to the heart of the matter. It made me think hard about things. I could dig that.

"Nothing. I don't want to hurt him."

"You can't be the rock and the river, Sam."

The pain behind my eyes returned so suddenly, I lost my breath. "Why did you say that?"

"I'm sorry," Leroy said, rubbing his forehead with his fingertips. "Steve used to say that a lot.

"He told me the story, once," he said. "About a rock and a river, and a guy trying to make up his mind."

I returned to the window, putting my back to Leroy. The memories came then, in a sweet and sorrowful rush. Sitting curled up on Stick's bed when I was little, when he used to read me stories from his books before we went to sleep. How he let me turn the pages, and how he'd read my favorite parts over and over again, 'cause they were his favorite parts too.

I rested my forehead on the windowpane. Leroy's voice broke through my thoughts.

"At the end of his life, a man went to the riverside and tried to bargain with the gods for immortality. To teach him a lesson, they granted his wish, telling him he could live forever on that spot, either as the river, or the rock by the water's edge.

"The rock is high ground," he went on. "Solid. Immovable.

Sure." I let him tell me, but I knew the story. It was a part of me.

"The river is motion, turmoil, rage.

"As the river flows, it wonders what it would be like to be so still, to take a breath, to rest. But the rock will always wonder what lies around the bend in the stream."

"I want to be both," I whispered.

"So did he," Leroy said, suddenly behind me. "But when the story ends—"

"I know how it ends."

"Hmm," Leroy said. "And you're here now."

"Yes." Stick was gone, but his work remained. He'd left it up to me. I owed him that much, but more than that, I wanted it for myself. Not Stick's way, exactly. Tonight, I would go home, eat dinner with Father and Mama, and sleep in my own bed. In the morning, I would go to school. But from now on I would be with the Panthers.

I turned around. "You do what you have to do, right?" I had a lot to learn, but finally, I was ready to learn it.

Leroy smiled slightly as he studied me. I leaned against the window. The sun warmed my back through the glass.

"You sound just like him." Leroy shook his head and clapped my arm. "Just like him."

"I know," I said. I wanted it to be true. Maybe then Stick would be less gone. But I knew I could never be like him. Stick had an energy, a charisma that I would never have. Nor could I be like Father, so steady, so sure of his ways. For so long now, I'd felt torn between their worlds — so different, and yet so much the same.

All this time I'd thought Stick was the river, but he was a rock in his own way too. The river moves, but it follows a path. When it tires of one journey, it rubs through some rock to forge a new way. Hard work, but that's its nature. Standing in this room, I knew there were no promises ahead, no road map. I couldn't follow anymore.

I was the river. I was the one who would turn the corner and see what tomorrow held in store.

AUTHOR'S NOTE

SAM'S STORY IS FICTIONAL. HIS FAMILY, friends, and the people he encounters in his community are all made-up characters. However, his story does involve some real historical events and individuals, such as the Reverend Dr. Martin Luther King Jr., a well-known leader of the civil rights movement.

Sam's story takes place in 1968, which was a critical turning point in the civil rights movement. The struggle that Sam faces in the story is based on the real-life challenges that many teenagers went through.

The Civil Rights Movement (1955–1968)

The civil rights movement began in the 1950s, when black Americans united to protest decades of racial discrimination and inequality. The Reverend Dr. Martin Luther King Jr. emerged early in the movement as a powerful leader. His passionate sermons and speeches motivated black communities to stand up for equal treatment under the law.

Dr. King joined with clergy, community leaders, student groups, and thousands of others to fight for civil rights. They believed that nonviolent "passive resistance" was the best way to oppose discriminatory laws. They took to the streets of cities all over the country, staging marches and demonstrations to make their goals known.

One of the first demonstrations, the Montgomery Bus Boycott, was a protest against segregation (separate seating areas for black riders and white riders) on public transportation. Black workers in Montgomery, Alabama, stopped riding the city buses. They refused to pay for a service that treated them as second-class citizens. The boycott lasted over a year. Finally, the city agreed to desegregate the buses.

The March on Washington for Jobs and Freedom, held on August 28, 1963, became the biggest demonstration that had ever been held in the United States. Hundreds of thousands of Americans, of all races, gathered around the Lincoln Memorial that day. Dr. King delivered his now-famous "I Have a Dream" speech.

Most demonstrations occurred on a much smaller scale. Sit-ins were especially common in segregated areas of the south. On February 1, 1960, four black college students staged a sit-in at the "whites only" section of a Woolworth lunch counter in Greensboro, North Carolina. The staff refused to serve them, so the students simply sat there for hours, occupying the chairs and waiting to be either served or arrested. They went back every day for six months, until Woolworth officially desegregated their lunch counter. Similar lunch-counter protests occurred all over the South. The protesters sometimes had condiments dumped on their heads or were beaten by other patrons in the restaurant.

The civil rights movement's most peaceful demonstrations were often met with violence. Black activists were often arrested, threatened, beaten, and even killed. At times the attackers included police and law enforcement officials, who used powerful firehoses to drive back the crowds and turned their police dogs loose on protestors. Integrated buses carrying black and white students were bombed by angry supporters of segregation.

The civil rights movement's philosophy of nonviolence meant that protestors should never fight back when attacked. They wanted to prove that hatred could be defeated by embracing peace and equality. But as the movement went on, it became harder for some black people to believe that nonviolence was going to work.

On April 4, 1968, Dr. King was assassinated. That night, throughout the nation, riots broke out in urban black communities as young people vented their rage over the tragedy. For many youth, Dr. King's murder symbolized white America's rejection of the civil rights movement's goal of promoting equality through peace.

The Black Panther Party (1966–1982)

The Black Panther Party for Self-Defense was founded in Oakland, California, in October 1966 by Huey Newton and Bobby Seale. The two college students were frustrated by the slow progress of civil rights legislation at creating actual change in the areas where it was most needed. They began monitoring police action in urban black communities. They believed that balancing the power dynamic between police and citizens would decrease police brutality. They formed teams who followed police officers through the streets to observe any encounters. The Panther teams openly carried large rifles, which was legal under California law. They would approach the police, while armed, if they believed the officers were stepping out of line.

The group later shortened its name to the Black Panther Party, to focus on a broader range of issues. The Party's ten-point platform outlined their goals, which they summed up by saying, "We want land, bread, housing, education, clothing, justice, and peace." They called for the release of black men from prison, exemption from military service for blacks, and fairer trials by jury for the accused.

These goals resonated with young blacks across the country. By 1969, the organization had more than five thousand members, and dozens of major cities had opened chapters of the Black Panther Party. The Party's militant aspects tapped into the frustration, anger, and determination felt by youth at the time, but violence was not at the core of their ultimate goals. All members attended political education classes, which included lessons in black history, politics, civil rights, justice, and the socialist theories of Mao Tse-tung, Che Guevara, Frantz Fanon, and Karl Marx. The Panthers sought to completely transform the social, political, and economic structures of the country.

The Panthers rejected "passive resistance" in favor of self-defense and self-determination. They believed it was up to black communities to demand equality, defend their rights, and look out for their own needs. The Black Panther Party initiated landmark community organizing efforts to bring much-needed services into black neighborhoods. Their programs included free neighborhood health clinics, drug-awareness education, GED classes, clothing supply, tutoring, legal aid and referrals, free dental care, free ambulances, bussing families to visit loved ones in prison, and free breakfast programs for school-age children.

Mainstream American culture was shocked by the Panthers' radical ideology and their militant approach to securing justice for black Americans. Law enforcement agencies grew nervous about the developing power base in black urban ghettoes. The Federal Bureau of Investigation created a counterintelligence program specifically to undermine black militant organizations like the Black Panther Party. They imprisoned, assassinated, or otherwise destroyed the reputations of many Party leaders.

The Party struggled under the pressure from law enforcement and the violence that resulted from it. Internal disputes grew, and the Party lost its cohesion. With many of its leaders dead, in prison, or in exile, the organization began fading in the late 1970s. The Panthers continued to promote their political agenda, but the community programs closed as membership declined. In 1982, the Black Panther Party officially disbanded.

ACKNOWLEDGMENTS

I AM BLESSED TO BE SURROUNDED BY THE LOVE and support of family, friends, and colleagues. Special thanks to Kobi, my brother and best critic, and to my parents, whose belief in me has never wavered.

Thanks to my friends, who faithfully cheer my successes and whose enthusiasm helps me persevere, including: Katherine Gebhardt, Kerry Land, Stephanie Nichols, Sarah and Christos Badavas, Ruth and Julian Schroeder, Pamela Harkins, and Kristina Leonardi.

Thanks to my writers groups for many valuable insights and indispensable advice; and to the faculty and students of Vermont College of Fine Arts, who nurtured this book from the very beginning, especially Ellen Levine, Tim Wynne-Jones, Liza Ketchum, Jane Resh Thomas, Bethany Hegedus, and my fellow MVPs of the July 2005 graduating class.

Finally, deepest thanks to Kate Angelella for embracing this story and giving it a home at Simon & Schuster.

KEKLA MAGOON

has worked with youth-serving non-profit organizations in New York City and Chicago. She holds an MFA in Writing for Children from the Vermont College of Fine Arts and resides in New York City. You can visit Kekla at her website: keklamagoon.com.